P9-CEZ-848

It's The Talk Of The Town

Nero's Movers and Shakers React To

You Can't Go Wrong
Stories from Nero, New York and Other Tales
By Bob Cudmore

"Bob is a hopeless, liberal apologist for the do-gooders and welfare cheats who infest this falling-down city. However, if I were you I'd buy this book because he has ME in it. As usual, Bob JUST DOESN'T GET IT!"
MIKE VAN WILSON, talk show host, WNRO Radio

"If I still owned the hardware store, I'd put Bob's book by the ice melt and car windshield scrapers, a real high traffic area. Thanks for putting me in the book, Bob."
LOU LARRAWELL, former Nero merchant

"Although he downplays what women have done for Nero, at least Bob is putting our city on the map. I know he wants to make money with this book and I can't blame him for that."
WANDA TAMBURINO, political operative

"I've known Bob and his family for many years and would consider it a personal favor if you were to buy his book."
MARTY THE BULL, retired Nero union leader

"Mr. Cudmore's writing style is as comprehensible as it is simplistic. He is dying to have someone say this, so I will: Bob Cudmore is the Garrison Keillor of the Rust Belt."
DON LESOCK, columnist, *Nero Nation*

"At this price for Bob's book, you can't go wrong."
DISEASE COTTER, retired mill worker

To Mary
for her constant love and
endless enthusiasm.

LEGEND
Map of the City of Nero
(And Village of Keepthemundaville)

1   Four Clover Tavern
2   Joe's Kitchen
3   Abandoned sock mills
4   Bowling alleys
5   Mostly vacant downtown mall
6   Hotel built in urban renewal days   .
7   Big downtown church
8   Church of St. Adalbartio
9   Sons of St. Adalbartio
10 WNRO
11 Nero Nation
12 Creek Diner
13 Wendy's
14 Nero First National Bank
15 Larrawell's Hardware
16 Formerly Waldorf's Stationers
17 Defunct sock museum
18 Abandoned railroad station. The last train was in 1971.
19 Cemetery Hill
20 Ethnic cemetery
21 Our hill. Home to workers and ethnic groups
22 The other hill. Home to pillars of society
23 Underutilized industrial park
24 Kmart, Wal-Mart, Home Depot
25 Nero Aerodrome
26 Country club
27 Olde Village Shoppes
28 Cul-de-sacs
29 Nero High School
30 Golden Arches

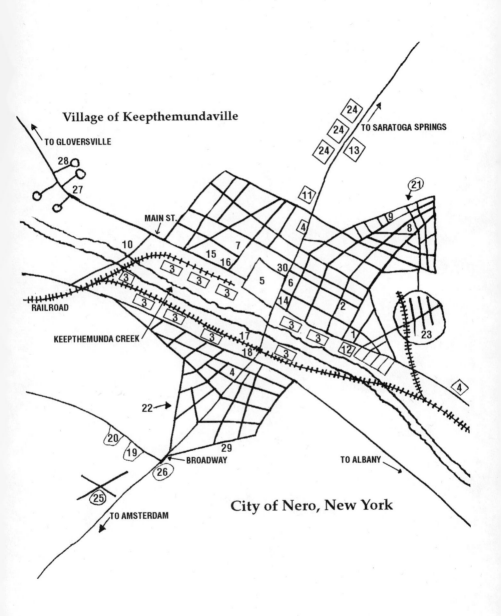

Village of Keepthemundaville

TO GLOVERSVILLE

28
27

MAIN ST.

10

RAILROAD

KEEPTHEMUNDA CREEK

22

20
19

26 BROADWAY

25

TO AMSTERDAM

24
24
24 13
TO SARATOGA SPRINGS

11

21

4

9
8

7
15
16

30
5   6

3
3
3

3
3

14

3

2

3
3

1

12

17

18   3

4

29

4

23

TO ALBANY

City of Nero, New York

You Can't Go Wrong

You Can't Go Wrong
Stories from Nero, New York and Other Tales
By Bob Cudmore

Illustrations by Jeanne A. Benas
Entering City of Nero, page 4; Bob Cudmore at Joe's Kitchen, page 10;
Disease Cotter at the Four Clover Tavern, page 15; Disease Cotter at the Nero Bowl, page 18;
Yarnworth Graves at Cemetery Hill, page 27; Hayden Waldorf, page 29;
Carla Gonzalez, page 36; Marty the Bull in Keepthemundaville, page 39;
Don Lesock at the *Nero Nation,* page 42; Lou Larrawell, page 46; Wanda Tamburino, page 58;
Mike Van Wilson at WNRO, page 61; Leaving City of Nero, page 84

Book design, cover design and typesetting by Chloe Van Aken
Type faces used for this book: ITC Berkeley, **Americana**, Helvetica Condensed

Published by: Nero Publishing Company, PMB 107, 123 Saratoga Road, Glenville, New York 12302
All rights reserved. No part of this book may be reproduced or transmitted in any form or by any means,
electronic or mechanical, including photocopying, recording or by any information storage and retrieval system without written permission from the author, except for the inclusion of brief quotations in a review.

Copyright © 2000 by Bob Cudmore
Illustrations Copyright © 2000 by Jeanne A. Benas

Printed in the United States of America by Coneco Litho Graphics, Inc., of Glens Falls, New York

ISBN 1-929529-02-3 (hardcover edition)
ISBN 1-929529-03-1 (softcover edition)

Library of Congress Catalog Card Number: 99-97773

DISCLAIMER
Nero is a fictional city and the characters, incidents and dialogues that take place in the fictional city of Nero
and its environs are products of the author's imagination and are not to be construed as real. Any resem-
blance to actual events or persons, living or dead, is coincidental.

You Can't Go Wrong

CONTENTS

From right,
Clarence and
Julia Cudmore,
Gladys Cudmore
Morrell 1949

Arlene Cudmore,
1988

❧

An Upstate Upbringing

To Clarence, Julia, Arlene and Vera Cudmore

We shouldn't take our memories for granted. When my father was in a nursing home, he and I had many conversations about his old job as a carpet weaver. He had worked at the Mohawk mill in Amsterdam, New York, from the 1930s until they closed his part of the mill in the 1970s.

That was a long time ago, he said, maybe six months. I told him, "Dad — they closed the mill twenty years ago."

We went on to talk about other things. If we didn't discuss the mill, we usually talked about his boyhood home or something he wanted that moment — a soft cookie, perhaps, a trip to the bathroom or a shave.

A few minutes later, father spoke up, "If what you say is true, that they closed the mill twenty years ago, what did I do for those twenty years?"

I told him how he cared for his wife, his house and his grandchildren. "Do you remember, you used to throw balsa airplanes on the garage roof with Robbe and you taught Kathleen arithmetic. We laid the carpet in Gladys and Vera's apartment. And we'd go on vacations together."

I don't know if he understood, or remembered.

Father was a mixture of poetry, agitation and zest for life in his last few months. Shortly before he passed away, he told his nurse, "My heart is hurting and I want to die." He also told my sister, "Bring me my hat, I want to die." As a man of his generation, he loved to wear a hat — a cap to work, a fedora to church.

1

His generation came of age in the Roaring 20s, Great Depression and World War II. Born in Torrington, England, in 1909, father came to America with my grandmother, aunts and uncles in 1912 in the steerage section of the Cunard liner *Majestic*. Grandfather had crossed over in 1909, offered work as a silk weaver at Fownes' mill in Amsterdam, operated by fellow immigrants from Britain.

One family story is that grandmother, who didn't want to go to America, delayed her family's departure several times, in the process saving their skins by failing to confirm tickets for the ill-fated *Titanic*.

Settling on Eagle Street in Amsterdam's teeming East End, our family became part of an ethnic mosaic that Kirk Douglas, Eagle Street's most famous resident, has called a United Nations of last names — Demski, Carbonelli, Rimkunas, Fratangelo, Schedlbauer, Allen and Cudmore.

Amsterdam's working life then revolved around the mills and social life revolved around taverns and houses of worship. My grandfather frequented the taverns and my parents met at church.

My mother, Julia Cook Cudmore, was born west of Amsterdam in rural Randall, where her father managed the country store. He died when mother was three and my grandmother held on in Randall during the Great War, feeding soldiers who guarded the town's Erie Canal lock against saboteurs. Young Julia was a great favorite of the soldiers, who called her the Queen of Randall. It may be that she was never quite so happy ever again.

When the war ended, Grandma Cook moved her family to Amsterdam's East End, where she ran a boarding house on Forbes Street. Though Grandma Cook was a strait-laced and God-fearing woman, her feeding and sometimes housing unmarried men did not go unnoticed.

Mother met father when he ushered at the former East Main Street Methodist Episcopal Church. They were married there in 1934 by a minister named Reverend Love; father was 25 and mother was 21.

Good-looking, humorous, hard working, musical and temperamental, my parents were married for 60 years, a testament to the triumph of common sense over aspiration. Both worked in the mills. Mother was a sewing teacher for awhile; their lives were routine. Father would have loved to sing for a living and mother was frustrated by her underused intelligence and what she saw, in her bitter moods, as her diminished lot in life. At the end of most days, however, both realized that their life together was a fairly comfortable one that neither was willing to abandon. My fondest memories are of overhearing their nightly in-bed conversations, gossiping about friends and relatives like two teen-agers.

My sister Arlene arrived in 1935 and I was born in 1945, making Arlene at first another mother to me. Arlene's greatest attribute was her ability to lavish affection on the people she loved. Arlene was also the first member of our family to break out of the mill town mold. Over mother's objections, Arlene went to college and used the family musical gift to forge a career as a music teacher.

The family I came with is gone now, father, mother and sister dying at approximate two-year intervals starting in 1994. Clarence, Julia and Arlene all have contributed to the stories in this book. Arlene lived to see many of them published, and she and I spent many a joyful moment recalling the cadence of mill town speech, expressions we used frequently — you can't go wrong, I don't blame you, it never fails.

My surviving link with the past is Vera Cudmore, father's

youngest sister, the first of our tribe born in America. A colorful character, Vera has been known to sign her greeting cards as "the old bat." When you ask her how she is, her response is always "Rotten." We meet most every Saturday in Amsterdam, gossiping and caring for each other as my parents did years ago.

❧

Guide to Nero, New York

The former sock-making capital of the world

INTRODUCTION

No one in Nero believes that anything good will ever happen again. Today, a declining upstate New York mill town, even Nero's beginnings were not auspicious. When the community was founded by British textile interests in the 19th century, the good classical names — Utica, Attica, Troy, Syracuse — had already been claimed by other upstate cities.

Some people thought the name Nero had a good, ancient ring to it, and noted that Nero rhymes with "hero." Nero also rhymes with "zero" and "Zero Nero" has become a common taunt aimed at the Nero High School basketball team when the Fiddlers run onto the court.

Nobody researched history when Nero was named and the connection with the infamous emperor Nero, who fiddled while Rome burned, wasn't discovered until the city's tenth anniversary. By then, the word Nero was lettered on the signs into town and had been carved in stone on a few public buildings. Residents decided to keep the name.

Sock-making was Nero's principal industry and, for many years, Nero was known as Sock City and "the sock-making capital of the world." In the 1960s, the sock mills abandoned Nero for cheaper labor down south and, ultimately, offshore. Nero has never recovered.

You Can't Go Wrong

Names to Know in Nero

Joe Cassidy, WNRO Radio Morning Host. "Please, not in my lifetime" is Joe Cassidy's signature putdown to callers with silly ideas, such as the woman who suggested Nero should change its name to Sock City to capitalize on its industrial past. When Joe encouraged listener calls suggesting new names for Nero, one caller proposed Government Check, given Nero's large percentage of people on Social Security and welfare, not to mention those working for the government.

Disease Cotter. A retired mill worker, Disease was a sickly child and given his lifelong nickname by heartless playmates. A regular at the Four Clover Tavern and Joe's Kitchen, Disease is a member of the Sons of St. Adalbartio. He occupies his time bowling, card playing and observing life in Nero.

Four Clover Tavern. Located in the basement of a building on a steep hill, the Four Clover is known affectionately as the Kneepad Inn — tipsy patrons crawl out on their knees to keep from sliding down the hill when they hit the street. The serious drinkers gather Saturday morning at the Four Clover for shots and beers.

Carla Gonzalez. Carla Gonzalez is a single mother, formerly on welfare, who now works three jobs to make ends meet. She opens the dry cleaners at the Nero downtown mall, styles hair at the Klever Kuts salon and does part-time deliveries for UPS.

Joe's Kitchen. Nero's most popular greasy spoon, Joe's Kitchen offers a "can't go wrong" daily special, including coffee and soft dessert, for $2.99.

Keepthemunda Creek. The Keepthemunda Creek provided water power for Nero's early mills. During the industrial heyday, the creek was dirty and smelly, sometimes running red or dark blue, depending on the dyes being used in the sock mills. Now that the mills have closed, the creek is cleaner. The creek's name derives from a Native American language and may mean "place of waters that flow" or "oppress the people."

KEEPTHEMUNDAVILLE. The most prosperous section of the town of Keepthemunda, located outside Nero. Keepthemundaville has advanced in population, business development and resident income as Nero has declined. The suburbanites pay a premium for flavored coffee and other necessaries at the Olde Village Plaza, where none of the shops accepts food stamps.

LOU LARRAWELL. Lou Larrawell did well in the hardware business, joined the country club and recently sold his business to a national chain. He ran afoul of Nero negativity when he tried to use some of his wealth to start a winter carnival. His motives were questioned by politicians and talk host Mike Van Wilson, who said: "Lou Larrawell is a fat cat who just doesn't get it."

DON LESOCK. Don Lesock writes a column for the local paper, *The Nero Nation.* He recently encouraged Nero to become a center for group homes for the mildly retarded, in light of opposition to such a group home in Glenville. Don's idea, which may have been satirical, was cautiously welcomed by one politician, ignored by suburbanites and viewed with skepticism by the retarded citizens organization.

MARTY THE BULL. A retired union leader in the Nero sock mills, Marty the Bull was a fearsome character in his day, known for taking care of his own. He now lives in Keepthemundaville, where his children have enjoyed many advantages. Marty's suburban neighbors keep him at arm's length.

NERO AERODROME. A small airport with a bumpy runway outside Nero. Like the Albany International Airport, the Nero Aerodrome has few international flights.

SONS OF ST. ADALBARTIO. An ethnic men's club, the Sons offer cheap food and drink to members and guests, card playing on weekend nights, a bowling team, an annual clambake and Christmas party. At the Christmas party, the waitresses wear blinking light corsages that play holiday tunes.

WANDA TAMBURINO. Wanda Tamburino is the office manager and constituent problem-fixer for Nero's popular congressman. Time spent trying to solve problems has given her a definite perspective on human nature: "With all the people I've helped, you would think I'd have it made if I went into business around here. But I wouldn't count on it. Nero people might pull a drowning woman from the creek, but she'd be on her own once they got her to shore."

HAYDEN WALDORF. Hayden Waldorf's family prospered in the stationery business when times were good in Nero. He was candid in the 1970s when Nero's downtown was gutted for an urban renewal project, saying: "Nobody knows if this is going to work but we have to do something and there's government money available." The 1970s renewal of Nero was fraught with poor ideas — an unpopular sock museum, a downtown hotel with a leaky roof and a parking garage prone to flooding.

MIKE VAN WILSON. Mike Van Wilson is the conservative host of "The Never Ending Argument" talk show on WNRO radio and self-proclaimed leader of the local battalion of outraged, grumpy old men. Mike hates Bill Clinton (the First Prevaricator), welfare cheats, the new immigrants and politicians "who just don't get it!"

WILLIAM AND EDGAR YARNWORTH. The Yarnworth brothers

came from England to found the sock mills, which defined the economic life of Nero for the first two-thirds of the 20th century. The Yarnworths and their offspring are buried on Cemetery Hill in two clusters of graves that reinforce the hierarchy of Nero's first family. It is as if an eternal board meeting has been called and William and Edgar, as usual, are at the head of the table.

≥≈

Stories from Nero, New York
Acknowledgments

The first Nero stories appeared from 1993 through 1995 as columns in the *Troy Record,* whose editors included Rex Smith, Lisa Robert Lewis and Charles Delafuente.

In 1996, Nero found a home at Brad Broyles' courageous Amsterdam paper, *The Star.* In 1997, Nero tales were printed in Tony Benjamin and Teresa Cuda's formidable Amsterdam paper, *The Free Press* of the *Mohawk Valley.* Neither *The Star* nor *The Free Press* exists today. I hope Nero had nothing to do with that.

Since 1996, Nero stories have appeared in the opinion section of *The Sunday Gazette* in Schenectady, edited by Art Clayman.

Several radio-related Nero tales have been reprinted in the national talk radio magazine *Talkers,* edited by Michael Harrison.

I am grateful to the editors who have printed the news from Nero and am particularly indebted to Art Clayman, who has given Nero its widest audience and whose suggestions have made the stories easier to read.

Special thanks also go to Ruth Peterson of Alplaus, B. John

Jablonski of Hagaman and Lewis Carosella of Rotterdam Junction for permission to reprint their articles, which responded to Nero stories.

Illustrations are by the accomplished artist Jeanne A. Benas of Latham. Photographs were provided by the Walter G. Elwood Museum, Montgomery County Department of History and Archives, Elmer Rossi, Jr., and Mrs. Joseph Urbelis. Book and cover design are by Chloe Van Aken.

&.

You Can't Go Wrong

Everyone in Nero loves a deal

A popular phrase in Nero is "You can't go wrong." A person might say: "You get meat loaf, mashed potatoes, string beans, coffee, and a soft dessert for $2.99. You can't go wrong." Even if the meat loaf is tasteless, the potatoes pasty, the beans soggy, the coffee bitter and the Jello tough, it's still a deal. Everyone in Nero loves a deal.

Working piecework in the Nero sock mills made the people appreciate quantity, as opposed to quality. Upstaters admire large quantities, just as the sock mill foremen used to admire higher production. The good sock weavers made better socks, but the guys who turned out more socks were the ones who had the most money to spend at the Four Clover Tavern after work.

One place where a Nero-ite enjoys a bargain is at a drinking establishment. The city has several ethnic clubs, men's clubs mainly, where the primary functions are to provide secluded places, as much as possible off-limits to the wives, where members gamble, drink and eat decent food at a good price. If a member of the Sons of St. Adalbartio wins a pot in a poker game, he can treat the whole table to drinks for under ten dollars. A member can take somebody for lunch on Guest Friday and get two beers, two hot dogs and fries for three dollars. You know what I'm thinking — You can't go wrong.

Also, you can't go wrong at a Nero rummage sale. A coat that costs two bucks is still a coat, even if it has a questionable odor.

In Nero, of course, there are a lot of ways you can go wrong and your fellow Nero-ites are more than happy to point out your foolishness. You probably paid too much for your car or paid the guy who moonlights from the fire department too much to put asphalt siding on your house. Nobody in Nero likes to be seen as a person who wastes money. We are very closed-mouthed about money in Upstate New York. We tell our friends details about family, sickness, even sex, but how much money do we have? Usually, folks change the subject.

Even though Nero is pretty decrepit, the banks seem to flourish and the story is that banks in Nero have more on deposit per capita than banks anywhere in the state. Some of the really suspicious old timers have literally hidden their loot at home.

Saving money became an obsession with immigrant Nero-ites because they came here with nothing and, when many of them got here, the Depression was underway or was a potent memory.

To this day, you don't find too many recyclable soda cans in the park where the Nero old-timers hang out.

I can hear one of the guys now: "Five cents just to walk a can over to the Stewart's? Hey, you can't go wrong!"

&

Christmas In Nero

Garish decorations and boisterous
conviviality save the holidays

The Christmas song that brings back the old days in downtown Nero is *Silver Bells*. As the song says, downtown Nero's sidewalks were busy in the holiday season. Much of Nero's happiness is in the past.

In the old days, the Nero 5 & 10 had big styrofoam snowmen and glitter-spattered white cotton snow in its windows. The real department store windows were elaborately decorated with moving Santas, elves and teddy bears. People thronged Main Street.

Unlike today's indoor malls, if there was snow, the Main Street shopping area became slushy because you had to go outside when you went from store to store. You felt the elements more when you shopped in downtown Nero and dressed for the weather. That probably cut down on the time you spent inside each store, given the quantity of clothing you were wearing.

We enjoyed lunch at the counter of the 5 & 10, even though the yellow gravy on the turkey dinner had an odd color. The gravy tasted all right but the color was something not found in nature.

One good thing about winter in Nero was that the polluted Keepthemunda Creek didn't stink as it did in the summertime.

The word "homeless" was not part of the vocabulary in the old days but there were beggars downtown. One man, with only one leg, had a regular spot next to the 5 & 10 where he sat selling pencils. An upstanding, church-going lady once confided that she wanted to kick the man with the one leg. Seeing adversity close-up can bring out the worst, even in December.

The barrooms did a brisk business and were always decorated for the holidays. Even the really awful joints managed to look good in December. Colored lights, a lighted Santa or two and early sunsets made all the difference. The men and women who worked in the factories spent more time than normal in the taverns during the long nights of the holiday season, often to the chagrin of their families.

Taverns were a major part of the social life of Nero in its industrial prime. When the factories let out, people would pour out of the mills like a river. Little branches would break off to go to their flats. Other streams of people would head for various barrooms.

Most taverns in Nero were on hills because the whole town was built on hills. The Four Clover Tavern, a basement tavern halfway up a steep hill, is still in business. Some continue to call the Four Clover the Kneepad Inn, the story being that the more tipsy patrons crawl out on their knees, so they won't roll down the hill when they hit the street.

Years ago, people didn't worry about drinking and driving because most people didn't drive to the barrooms. They walked. The drinking caused some terrible fights, just like today. People weren't as well-armed so they didn't kill or maim each other as often. And, most of the factory workers were proud that they almost always went to work and put in a full day, despite their drinking.

There were many characters in the old Nero taverns — like Stan, the former Four Clover bartender. He always called you by name and told you not to slip on the ice on the way out. Even if you had slipped back then, you probably wouldn't have sued him. There was Silent Ike, who sat on a bar stool, drank and didn't say a word. Ike was sweet on one of the ladies in the bar and used to buy her whatever she mentioned. If she said she needed a stamp for a letter, Ike brought her a whole roll of stamps the next night. Another character was Smiling Frank, the resident curmudgeon. Whatever it was, he had seen better. "Nice day, Frank," you'd tell him. "I've seen better," was the reply.

Of course, let's not get too misty about the old days on the tavern scene. The attitude of the general population toward heavy drinking may have been more tolerant, but drinking took its toll.

This year, I joined my old friend Disease Cotter at the annual holiday party at his men's club, the Sons of St. Adalbartio, which was dec-

DISEASE COTTER

orated with cheap silver and gold garlands and fake greenery. The waitresses wore blinking light corsages that played holiday tunes. The garish decorations and boisterous conviviality did a great deal to keep spirits bright at this time of year, which can be gloomy for some.

Disease said, "The Veterans Club used to host a children's Christmas party which I always went to when I was young. A lot of poor kids got some nice toys at that party. On Christmas Eve, my aunts and uncles used to come to our house after spending time at the Four Clover Tavern, where there was plenty of holiday cheer. My mother was not one for drinking and usually had some comment to make. It made for a lively gathering.

"People went to church, of course. In the church that we attended we always used candles Christmas Eve. When you came in to sit down they gave you lighted candles. The choir, which had more than one or two members with failing eyesight, would march into the darkened church, balancing hymn books and lighted candles while they sang 'Joy to the World.' It's a wonder somebody didn't trip and start a fire."

As for New Year's Eve, while Albany, Saratoga, Amsterdam and Gloversville have had First Night celebrations, the concept of a community-wide, family-friendly, arts-centered way to celebrate New Year's Eve has not taken hold in Nero. In fact, Nero still offers a scaled-down version of what it was that First Night replaced.

In the old days, when factory work was steady and plentiful, people in Nero regarded New Year's Eve as what you might call last night. New Year's Eve was your last chance during the holiday season to tie on a load before the mill opened again the day after tomorrow.

"Maybe I'll go to First Night in Saratoga on New Year's Eve but I'll probably end up back at the Four Clover or at the Sons," Disease said. "It'll be the regular crowd and kind of cozy. The Nero bar scene is not what it was but it's better than nothing. In fact, that guy at the end of the bar reminds me of our old friend Smiling Frank. Nice day, isn't it, buddy?"

ه

Nero Bowled Over by the Arrival of Spring
Bowling has helped define life in Nero

In Nero, we do things differently than people in more upscale areas, even in the way we officially mark the passing of the seasons. During the cold weather months, my friend Disease Cotter plays cards every Friday night at his men's club, the Sons of St. Adalbartio. Since the bowling season began in the fall, every one of the Friday night card players has contributed $2 a week toward the cost of a spring banquet.

The connection between the card game and the bowling season puzzled me. Many of the card players bowl, of course, but some don't. Even Disease, a veteran kegler, strained his back shoveling snow from his driveway into the street and has not been a regular bowler this season.

"Everyone knows when the bowling season starts and when it ends," Disease explained. "So we always pick those dates to start and stop our banquet collection."

The league bowling season in Nero, you see, is sacred, something like Ramadan in Moslem nations, the High Holy Days in Israel or Lent in Catholic countries.

Bowling has helped define life in Nero. Even though bowling,

DISEASE COTTER

like everything else, has declined, the sport is still important. Good bowlers generally get more regular and better press than the politicians and the bowlers don't have to make appearances at wakes and ribbon-cuttings to maintain their status as local celebrities.

To everything there is a season. There is a time to bowl and a time to put the bowling ball in the closet, next to the ice-fishing gear.

Disease and his friends have their banquet in April, collecting more than $30 per man. That's enough money for more fun than you want to know about at the Four Clover, or even at a more expensive restaurant, one that treats chicken wings as an appetizer and not a main course, for example.

After a persistent winter, people in Nero are glad to see the end of bowling season, the end of winter card games. Winter is, by and large, the most depressing time in Nero, where the buildings are not quaint but functional. Nero's buildings keep out the elements but do not improve the landscape. More painted tires than designer flags line the city's streets.

Nero in winter is the kind of dismal Upstate New York community that makes travelers glad to reach Lenox, Stockbridge or other quaint New England places, where shops are scented with bayberry candles and more homes are covered with clapboard than with asphalt siding.

The hot dog stand outside of Nero opens in April, another sign of spring, giving people a new spot to grab a reasonably priced meal, if they don't want to sit inside the dingy Four Clover Tavern on a bright sunny day.

New leaf growth on the trees is finally giving some blessed cover to the more run-down parts of Nero. Life is good or, at least, better than it was when spring is here.

ಎ

Summer in Nero
When the creek used to smell

A sickening and distinctive smell used to come from the Keep-themunda Creek that runs through Nero, the former sock-making capital of the world. When the sock mills were running full tilt, industrial waste went into the creek in a steady stream. Now that the mills are closed, the Keepthemunda doesn't smell, even in the summer.

Back in the good old summertime in Nero, the sock mills were awfully hot places to work. The valley air was stagnant and few people had air conditioning.

People who could afford to rented camps in the Adirondacks for a week, usually during the annual mill shutdown, right after the Fourth of July. It was an effort to take everything to camp for such a short time, but that was what the working person could afford.

In Nero itself, people sat on their porches or in front of their houses on hot summer nights — the men in undershirts and the women wearing little as possible. People sat on kitchen chairs. If the lawn chair had been invented, it had not made its way to Nero.

Whatever the young people were doing — riding bikes or playing kickball in the street — some older people didn't like it. Some members of every generation see no redeeming features in the next crop. And, there are always some youngsters willing to torment their elders.

Roadhouses were popular warm weather destinations for Nero's teens in the days of the 18-year-old drinking age. Putting a tavern near the woods off a secluded country road added to alcohol's already substantial appeal. There were drunken drivers and more than a few accidents.

Summer was a time when young people tried out adult vices — smoking, drinking and sex. Cars were favorite spots for sex, as were the woods around the roadhouse.

"Because I was friends with the Mayor's daughter, I used to work summers for the Nero Department of Public Works," my old friend Disease Cotter recalled as we enjoyed an ice cream cone the other day at the Kreme 'n Kone right outside Nero. "Sometimes we worked hard for the city and other times we hid out from nosy citizens and aldermen. If you worked the early garbage collection shift, you got off work in time to get to the track in August.

"One morning, my friend Jim and I sneaked into a little shed at the DPW garage just before roll call for the day's assignments. We were worn out from a binge at the roadhouse the night before and thought we'd nap for a few minutes. We didn't wake up until after lunch time. One of the foremen was still at the DPW garage when we stumbled out of the shed.

"The foreman was mad but knew he'd get blamed along with us for our missing roll call. He had us sweep the garage until everybody came back, like that was what he had planned for us to do that day all along."

When it was really hot when I was a kid, my mother would make iced tea. She brewed tea in a big metal pot, added lemon and sugar while the tea was still hot. She put the ice in just before dinner. The sight of that pot cooling on the counter was a welcome sign when I came in from riding my bike on hot summer evenings.

When Ma made iced tea, I could drink that along with the

grownups. If it was cool enough for coffee for the grownups, though, my folks wouldn't let me drink coffee, I had to drink milk. To this day, I love iced tea. Some vices are more defensible than others.

ॐ

All It Takes Is a Dollar and a Dream

Nero had many places where people went in,
but never came out

M any people in Nero hope the government will make it possible for their city to have a casino. A casino could revitalize the nearly empty downtown mall, although critics say a casino would bring false hope and trouble to a city that has had more than its share of failed ventures and broken dreams.

The State Lottery, Off Track Betting, and Bingo are very popular in Nero. Nero even has an historical claim as a gambling center.

Before the state became so involved in games of chance, illegal gambling was almost a profession in Nero. Certainly, it was more than a pastime.

When people saw you on the street in the morning , they didn't ask about the weather, they asked cryptically "What came out?" The illegal numbers game was huge in the sock mills. Three digit numbers were written on each date of the wall calendars in barbershops.

Every factory floor had its numbers taker. If you won, your guy would stop by your flat with your winnings, cash of course. The old bookmakers gave better odds than the state does with the Lottery, but there was a price paid for gambling in old Nero.

An uncle of mine worked as a runner for the bookies and had a bad habit of not always placing the bets people made with him. Cash in hand, the lure of a couple of shots at the Four Clover Tavern was strong for Uncle Yates. Most times, the horses didn't come in and nobody was the wiser.

Once, my uncle was supposed to place a bet for a local housewife. He didn't, the horse finished first and the housewife went to the Nero cops to have my uncle arrested! The cops told her: "Look, lady, if we arrest him, we gotta arrest you. This whole thing is illegal." The fact that the housewife thought the police should regulate illegal gambling showed how normal and legitimate the enterprise seemed to be.

Occasionally, the State Police would raid the bookies and the State Police tried to keep the Nero Police from knowing about it. Telling the Nero Police would have been like taking an ad in the paper.

After one State Police raid, the Nero Police Chief spoke on the local radio station, in his daily report on who was arrested for what, and kept repeating: "This was a State Police raid. Nero police knew NOTHING, I emphasize we knew NOTHING about this raid."

People who grew up in Nero were surprised to go to little shops in other cities that really were what they were supposed to be. Many newsstands, shoe repair shops, candy stores and the like in Nero were fronts for bookie joints. From the number of newsstands in Nero, you would have thought it was the most well-read city in the state.

Nero was full of places with dark windows where men went in but never seemed to come out. In fact, one complaint about Nero's new Off Track Betting parlor in the downtown mall is that wives and and other interested parties can peer inside through the spacious windows and see who's gambling.

One place in the old days that took numbers sold ice cream. If strangers were in the store, people placed their bets by ordering SIX vanillas, THREE chocolates and TWO strawberries, or whatever.

One local story was that somebody once brought a pair of shoes to Otto the Shoemaker. Otto didn't fix shoes, of course, but ran his book in a shop that had some shoemaking gear. He sent the shoes out to be fixed.

There is both a great appeal and great danger in gambling, as strong as the appeal and danger of the other controversial preoccupations of many Nero-ites — drinking and sex.

Years ago in Nero, people squandered the money they made in the sock mills with the bookies. Today, many Nero-ites are on public assistance and people think differently of using welfare money to gamble.

Even though the economic good that casinos will bring is probably overstated, gambling profits can be put to good use. The State Lottery helps pay for the government and some parochial schools are kept afloat by bingo. Some of the loudest critics of the expansion of casino gambling come from Saratoga County. If you ask me, it takes monumental gall for people who have benefited mightily from a racetrack to oppose another kind of gambling.

If Nero gets a casino, I'll probably go there at least once. It's part of my past and, hey, you never know.

≥▲

The View from Cemetery Hill
Hard times at the cemetery

The best view of Nero is from Cemetery Hill. During late May and June, the small valley of the Keepthemunda Creek below the cemetery bursts with glowing shades of green. Even the abandoned sock mills look halfway decent from this elevated perspective.

On Cemetery Hill, Nero's mill-owning families — the Waldorfs, Foots and Yarnworths — share their final resting space with many of their less affluent Protestant employees. Nero has separate cemeteries, of course, used by Catholics and Jews.

The Waldorfs and the Foots maintain large mausoleums which look like Greek temples. The Yarnworths have adopted a burial style that is less ostentatious but more awe-inspiring. There are two symmetrically arranged clusters of graves where descendants of the Yarnworth brothers — William and Edgar — are buried. The effect of the grave clusters is to reinforce the hierarchy of Nero's first family. It is as if an eternal board of directors meeting has been called and William and Edgar, as usual, are at the head of the table.

The Yarnworths came from England to found an industry that defined the economic life of Nero for the first two-thirds of this century. Whether they are spinning in their graves witnessing Nero's decline of the past three decades is a matter of frequent local conjecture.

Nero's mill town heyday was in the past, and donations to maintain Cemetery Hill have dwindled. Ironically, one effect has been to make the cemetery as difficult to enter as an upper class fraternal lodge. There are winding, rutted roads lined on each side by ditches that threaten to swallow visiting cars or even hearses. It is not an easy place for a funeral during winter or early spring.

Cemetery Hill is not nearly as well maintained as the nearby ethnic Catholic cemetery, which also boasts more elaborate floral displays. The glue that holds an ethnic group together apparently makes for more effective upkeep than the ties that bind Protestant entrepreneurs and their employees.

Floral tributes and American flags peak Memorial Day weekend at Cemetery Hill, then decline as summer begins and hot weather takes its toll. Many people visit the cemetery in the spring, summer and fall. The saddest visitors are the parents tending flowers around stones depicting their deceased children as little lambs, small angels, even an occasional teddy bear.

There are bereft widows, widowers, daughters and some sons who make gravestone beautification a working tribute to the deceased. They come with car trunks full of gardening gear — hoses, rakes, shovels and fertilizer. Some come every day.

Sixty years ago, the matriarch of one of Nero's Protestant immigrant families died an early, if expected death from what they used to call dropsy. The first piece of land this family owned in the New World was a burial plot.

With trolleys and buses, Cemetery Hill was an easy place to visit in the 1930s and 1940s and the family came often to pay respects to their mother. They usually spent the afternoon and brought a picnic lunch, which they enjoyed on the grass beneath huge shade trees.

The youngest grandson remembers playing hide and seek with his older sister among the trees, tombstones, flags and flowers. One mausoleum was built right into the side of a small hill and you could run up one side of the mausoleum and down the other. Why the older people were sometimes sad or angry in such an interesting place made no sense to that little boy.

ೋ

Urban Renewal Fails to Renew Nero
The sock museum was never a draw

Recently, government welfare programs for individuals have been reformed and restrained but welfare programs for businesses and communities have grown, if you are in the right place. People in Nero are sympathetic to a Glenville businessman who missed out on the government's business-welfare programs because of location, location, location.

Glenville restaurant owner Ralph Spillenger wondered why his inland Bayou Cafe on Route 50 — a family restaurant featuring spicy food and weekend entertainment — didn't qualify for low-interest loans and a grant, which were considered for people buying a cafe on the Mohawk River in Glenville. Government money is available to revitalize the riverfront. Route 50 in Glenville and Nero, for that matter, are not eligible.

"I wish I could get a three percent loan," Spillenger told the Glenville Town Council. Stan, Jr., the bartender/owner at the Four Clover Tavern in Nero, would agree. However, it's unlikely any aid will be forthcoming to repair the tan and torn asphalt siding on the Four Clover, even though the government appears flush with cash this year. There won't even be any grant money to fix up the neon sign, which currently flashes Fo r C over.

Nero feels cheated as government development programs ranging from riverfront projects in Glenville and Amsterdam to the Metroplex in Schenectady are announced. Nero doesn't qualify for riverfront aid because the city is built on the Keepthemunda Creek, not on a river. As for the Metroplex, Nero is simply not big enough, nor deprived enough to make another attempt at revitalization of its downtown a positive campaign promise for incumbent statewide and regional candidates in the next election.

Frankly, now that Schenectady County has jumped aboard the Metroplex bandwagon, folks in Nero don't know whether to envy or pity the Schenectadians.

When Nero's downtown was gutted to make way for urban renewal in the 1970s, longtime local businessman, Hayden Waldorf of Waldorf's Stationers, admitted privately that there is an element of blind-to-the-consequences risk in such a major undertaking — destroying a decrepit but still-functioning downtown that had defined Nero, for better or worse, for close to a century.

"Nobody knows if this project is going to make Nero any better,

HAYDEN WALDORF

don't let anybody kid you," Waldorf said back then. "But we have to do something and there's government money to to do this. Let's cash the check."

Nero's downtown has not prospered. The sock museum was never a draw. The flat roof of the downtown hotel leaked. The creek flooded the concrete parking garage, which would have been more of a problem if more cars had parked there.

Businessman Waldorf, whose support was crucial to Nero urban renewal twenty years ago, was a well-connected man, a real city father. He lived on the right hill, went to the right church, belonged to the proper service club, was married to a daughter of one of the founders of the local mills and was widely admired for his business sense, general integrity and common sense.

To hear him admit, even privately, that he hadn't a clue as to the feasibility of Nero's big development project of the 1970s, a project he supported, was a revelation.

There may not be any "smart money." It could be that nobody is really in the know about anything as complex as the future of city life.

≥▲

What's in a Name

Should Nero be renamed Government Check?

When North Tarrytown decided to call itself Sleepy Hollow, renaming fever came to Nero, the unfortunately named Upstate New York mill town whose aging buildings line both sides of the Keepthemunda Creek.

When Nero was developed by British textile interests years ago, the really good classical names like Utica, Attica and Syracuse had already been claimed by older upstate cities. Some people thought Nero had a good ancient ring to it, and noted that Nero rhymes with "hero."

Nero also rhymes with "zero," which has become a common taunt aimed at the Nero High School basketball team when the Nero Fiddlers run onto the court. "Zero Nero, Zero Nero, ZEEEE ROOOO NEE ROOO" the opposing fans yell at the start of each game. It's very unsettling.

Nobody thought to research history when Nero was named and no one discovered the connection with the infamous Roman emperor Nero, who fiddled while Rome burned, until the town's tenth anniversary. By then the name was on all the signs into town and had been carved in stone on the public buildings. Over the years, people have accepted the name. The Nero Fiddlers may not be the catchiest name for the high school sports teams, but at least Native Americans aren't offended. And today, there is a curmudgeonly faction against changing the name of Nero simply because the fiddling emperor connection seems appropriate, given the number of suspicious fires in the town's abandoned mill buildings.

Joe Cassidy, who hosts the morning talk show on WNRO radio, has been asking listeners for suggestions on a new name for Nero. Palm Springs and Sun Valley have shown surprising popularity. Callers say that, unlike North Tarrytown, Nero really has no claim to historical importance, so why not pick a name that gets your mind off the region's burdensome winter weather. Maybe that's how the Montgomery County town of Florida got its name.

One caller proposed Government Check as a good name, given Nero's large percentage of retired folks on Social Security, government workers and younger people on welfare.

Disgruntled old timers say the new name should be in a foreign language, since so many of the new immigrants don't speak English. One of the newcomers suggested the name Friendship, although you could clearly tell he thought that friendliness was a quality Nero-ites did not extend to newcomers.

Little Sin City was proposed to take advantage of Nero's old reputation as a wide open town for drinking, gambling and sex. More mainstream history buffs argued for the old Indian name of Keepthemunda or, they said, how about Sock City, to recall Nero's glory days when its sock mills were booming. Talk show host Joe Cassidy's rejoinder to that suggestion was his classic caller putdown: "Please, not in my lifetime."

After the subject took off as a talk show topic, a committee was formed to explore "the positive aspects of changing the name of our town, including more tourism, jobs and improved community spirit." Local politics being what it is, the committee is still arguing over what to name the committee.

"No matter what you call our town," one caller told Joe Cassidy on WNRO the other day, "It's still going to be Zero Nero. We're still going to be known as the town where the sock mills moved out, where the creek used to smell, the town that people in the classier suburbs avoid like the plague, a place to leave if you can and live in only if you have to."

Still, Sun Valley, New York, has a nice ring to it.

ᕆ

The Ajax Museum at WNRO

Notes from a nervous news director

The Keepthemunda Creek flows by the WNRO studios and transmitter in a swampy area of Nero. They build AM radio towers in wetlands to improve reception. On a clear day, though, you can barely hear WNRO on the other side of north Nero.

Back in 1965, when the big power blackout took place in the Northeast, many radio stations (WNRO included) didn't stay on the air because they didn't have generators. Maybe this was a precursor to the Y2K problem. In the late 1960s, the government offered to give radio stations generators if the stations built fallout shelters, usually underground.

WNRO still has the generator, which has been useful over the years in ice storms and the like. Since the subterranean fallout shelter was built next to the radio station near the swamp and the creek, it was always full of water. When you went down the ladder to the fallout shelter, you could peer in through a little window in the door and see radio equipment, tins of crackers and other nuclear war supplies floating in one, two or three feet of water. The Nero Fire Department pumped out the shelter two or three times a year.

The flooded fallout shelter was the butt of many jokes. Some said Jimmy Hoffa was buried there. When a new announcer was hired, the old hands would send him on some stupid errand down to the flooded fallout shelter.

They filled in the underground fallout shelter a few years ago. The new shelter is above ground and doubles as a storage area. At least they get some use out of it.

Somebody rescued a tin of crackers before the underground shelter was filled in and that tin was the start of the Ajax Museum at WNRO. The museum was named "Ajax" in honor of a radio comedy routine called "The Ajax Liquor Store."

The museum is in an abandoned washroom off the big room where the WNRO transmitter is located. The nutty announcers and weird engineers at WNRO began putting in all kinds of pointless exhibits:

— notes from the nervous news director;
— obscene tapes made by one of the part-time engineers;
— a crumpled piece of tin foil called the Nero Solar Heat Generator;
— a clock that runs backwards, dedicated to the FM station, which plays elevator music.

You wouldn't take a tour of Cub Scouts to see these things, but if the night disc jockey's cousin comes in from Detroit, the Ajax Museum is on the must-see list. Radio is fun.

&

You've Got to Take Care of Your Own
Marty the Bull's lament

Retired Nero union leader Marty the Bull is longing for the days when people took care of their own. Marty was holding forth at the Four Clover Tavern last Monday, during all-you-can-eat ravioli night. Years ago, Marty would have scared me — he was a big man with the union at the sock mills before the mills moved south. He was tough. On the plus side, Marty was a good person to know if your brother-in-law needed work at the sock mills to get through the winter.

Marty is older and not as awe-inspiring as he once was and, polishing off his ravioli at the bar of the Four Clover, he was lamenting how big shots don't take care of people anymore. Today, Marty said, with the sock mills gone and local stores swallowed by the chains, the only people who feel secure are those with the biggest protector of them all, the government.

But even some of the people who commute from Nero to Albany are worried that they might lose their jobs. "They've got to take care of their families," Marty said as he pounded the bar. I think I heard that line in a bad gangster movie, but Marty the Bull has a point.

Marty told this story: "My son doesn't get his haircut at Tony's barbershop, like I do, but goes to Carla, one of the hairstylists at Klever Kuts in the practically empty downtown Nero shopping mall. I think guys go to these women beauticians to flirt more than anything else, but that's beside the point."

Carla used to have a good job with the government in Albany but was laid off and is now working three jobs to make ends meet.

She opens the dry cleaners in the mall and works until she takes her kids to day care. She's a single mother. Then she works at the hair salon. She works part time for UPS on weekends. They say firms like that hire part-timers to work a few hours lifting boxes. The part-timers get real tired and then rest on their own time.

In any event, Carla is exhausted and still makes less with the three jobs than she made with her one government job, which gave her weekends off. Maybe she'd be better off on welfare and maybe that has occurred to her.

CARLA GONZALEZ

"Of course when I brought up this story at Tony's barbershop," said Marty, "Tony was mad that I was plugging a competitor who looks better than he does."

The old-timers started the usual complaints about kids today, welfare today, the new immigrants, and how tough things were in the Depression when people were glad to sweat ten or twelve hours a day in the mills.

"I tried to tell the guys that back in the old days you thought that somebody would look out for you," Marty said. "You went to the big shots who were your own people, or made nice to the right people, if your own people couldn't do much for you."

Today it's all bottom line, according to Marty. Groveling doesn't impress the current crop of bean counters, who are probably worried they are about to be replaced themselves.

Marty said: "These companies just can't expect to have everything their own way. What was it that playwright guy Arthur Miller wrote — you can't eat the orange and throw the peel away. A worker is not a piece of fruit."

When Marty the Bull starts quoting Arthur Miller, you know the day of judgment may soon be at hand.

ҙ҉

Keepthemundaville

There is a price to be paid for the absence of the poor

None of the shops at the Olde Village Plaza in Keepthemundaville accepts food stamps. No merchant in the Plaza uses a public address system, as big supermarkets do, so no one looking at clothing, gift items or liquor can be offended by hearing amplified announcements in a language different from English.

Keepthemundaville is the most prosperous section of the Town of Keepthemunda, located outside the City of Nero. As Nero has declined, Keepthemundaville has advanced in population, business development and resident income. Sometimes it seems that the only thing Nero and Keepthemundaville have in common is the creek which runs through both communities.

In Nero, the creek used to smell when the sock mills were running. The smell of the creek in the city, an odor that eventually dissipated when the mills moved south, probably hastened the departure of Nero's wealthier citizens to Keepthemundaville and other upstream locations.

Shoppers in Nero are inclined to buy the most inexpensive items at the big supermarkets right over the city line. However, those who frequent Olde Village Plaza in Keepthemundaville expect to pay more. It costs money to maintain outdoor flowerpots and covered walkways. There is a price to be paid for fresh paint, indirect lighting, and the absence of the poor. If you visit the Plaza regularly, you will hear that rents are high. You especially hear that when prices are being raised at the Olde Kitchen Cutlery Shoppe. Even the consignment shop (or shoppe, as it's also called) has ambience at the Plaza.

Those who were raised in Nero and fled their declining city for the suburbs are sometimes taken aback that a small coffee costs so much at the Village Bagel and Croissant Shoppe in the Plaza. Also, the coffee in the bright and cheery bagel shop comes in an array of flavors, unlike the cheaper regular coffee at the dingier and more boisterous Joe's Kitchen in Nero.

MARTY THE BULL

Like the noisy crowd at Joe's Kitchen, the people who still live in Nero's old neighborhoods are literally in each other's faces, admittedly not always a situation that buoys your faith in the human race. Nero can be an edgy and contentious place, especially in the summer. Those who live in Keepthemundaville, on the other hand, can choose to live in general ignorance of their neighbors, splendidly isolated in suburban homes surrounded by moat-like lawns.

Lawn care, especially in the spring, weighs heavily on married men who live in the suburbs. As the children move out and middle age advances unchecked, a second floor flat on one of the hills of Nero can seem preferable to a suburban home, at least from a maintenance point of view.

One early evening, I stopped to talk with Nero expatriate Marty the Bull while he struggled mowing his lawn in Keepthemundaville. A former union leader in the Nero sock mills, Marty made enough money by whatever means before the factories closed to move to the suburbs and, despite his difficulty with lawn care, he will remain there.

Marty has paid a ton in village taxes by now and his children received a good education at the Keepthemundaville Central Schools. Now grown, his children are doing well in the world. Marty also likes his split-level house, two-car garage, the fresh air and open space of the suburbs. Sometimes, Marty misses the old neighborhood.

"I knew everybody on the block when I lived in Nero; I used to be in their kitchens," Marty told me. He's only been in one neighbor's house since moving to the suburbs and Marty didn't make it to the kitchen, he only got as far as the garage.

In Keepthemundaville, you see the young kids breeze by on

their bikes and you see men and women, sometimes with young children, out walking. You hear the muffled thud of car stereos as the older kids drive by. You know what the husbands look like because they're out with their snowblowers or lawnmowers, depending on the season. Unless you have a history with the people you see, you nod and move on.

"Maybe it's all right," said Marty. "If we got to know each other real well, we'd get on each other's nerves. It'd be Nero all over again."

≈

Nero Opts for More Group Homes

Can Nero become Group Home Capital
of Upstate New York?

Unlike officials in other upstate cities, Nero's movers and shakers never thought for a minute that WMHT-TV would locate in their city. The Capital District's public television station ultimately rejected ridiculously lucrative overtures from Albany and Schenectady and decided to build its new, high-tech facility in Rensselaer County.

Although Nero was never under consideration as a location for the region's public television facility, there is a campaign of sorts to make Nero, not Glenville, the location for the region's next group home for mildly retarded people.

In sitting on their hands in the WMHT siting competition, Nero's frequently ill-advised politicians for once made the right decision. Why compete for something you know you won't get? Nero is

DON LESOCK

about as likely a site for a regional public television station as it is for the next Olympic Games or Emmy award show.

As for the controversy over locating a group home for mildly retarded adults in suburban Glenville, a Nero media icon is asking the region's retarded citizens organization to consider locating the next such group home in Nero, the former sock-making capital of the world.

As columnist Don Lesock put it in his twice-weekly column in the *Nero Nation:* "We never had a prayer of landing WMHT but we have a much better shot as the location for the next group home."

Lesock continued: "Why do we want a group home? Humanitarian reasons aside, let's go for something others don't want. This is akin to the advice to stock pickers to buy low and sell high.

"In fact, if Nero became the group home capital of Upstate New York, that would be a solid improvement in our situation. We have plenty of empty buildings and we won't mind increased traffic or noise. As for setting up a business in a residential area, most people in Nero, unlike our suburban neighbors, would be glad for any business that is willing to locate in this down-in-the-dumps place."

So far, the *Nero Nation* has printed three letters responding to this idea. As they always do, Nero's politicians read Lesock's column with interest but most came to the conclusion that the retarded citizens organization would not want to make Nero the group home capital of Upstate New York, preferring instead to house their clients in more affluent areas. However, one city council member wrote a letter to the editor suggesting the city apply for a demonstration grant to see if Nero could become a "group home cluster city," under state or federal economic development guidelines.

Just outside Nero, folks in suburban and prosperous Keepthemundaville were irked with the column, figuring Lesock was indirectly taking a shot at them. However, since it was possible the columnist was serious about getting group homes for Nero, nobody said anything about Lesock's idea Sunday morning at the Olde Village Plaza's bagel shop as the suburban neighbors exchanged small talk over coffee and carbohydrates. In general, discourse in Keepthemundaville is more genteel than in rough-and-tumble Nero, although residents of Keepthemundaville have not been put to the test of a group home on one of their cul-de-sacs.

A resident of Keepthemundaville did write a letter to the newspaper praising the positive effects on young people of family-oriented, single-family home neighborhoods but avoiding any direct reference to group homes.

Friends of the retarded citizens organization read Lesock's column for signs of political incorrectness that could be the basis of a finger-pointing letter. In the end, a rather balanced piece was sent to the editor from this faction, accusing Lesock of insensitivity ("Human beings are not like the stock market, Mr. Lesock") but promising not to ignore Nero in future siting decisions.

&.

Local Flavor Is Disappearing from Upstate Businesses

Lou Larrawell's days
as a bank director are numbered

When the franchise fast-food restaurants moved in to replace the mom-and-pop eateries in Nero, oldtimers were chagrined but quickly adapted. The grumpy old men who used to meet for breakfast at the Creek Diner now get together at the Golden Arches.

So what, they said, the Creek had lousy coffee and at least you can fit on the chairs at the fast-food place, instead of cramming four guys into one of the Creek's charming but tiny, painted wooden booths. And, if you want local color, they said, you can still go to Joe's Kitchen or even the Four Clover grill and get locally made, greasy food at bargain prices.

Then the Nero hardware, clothing, stationery and furniture stores shut down in the face of competition from out-of-town malls and big-box retailers like Wal-Mart, Kmart and Home Depot. So what, the shoppers said, a bargain is a bargain. You can't go wrong with Wal-Mart's prices.

Lou Larrawell's old hardware store in downtown Nero, to name one example, was overpriced, crowded and confusing, they said. From late summer to fall, it was hard to get at the screws, nails, nuts and bolts because of the lawn rakes that Lou leaned against the counter with old-fashioned, dangling price tags. Sure, Lou was friendly but he always closed on Saturday at noon and all day Sunday, making it hard when you ran out of paint Saturday afternoon.

Lou is one of the grumpy old men now and hears these complaints from his friends when they get together for coffee at the Golden Arches.

Although Lou was strictly retail, he had done well before he closed the store, joined the country club and a decent fraternal organization, regularly attended worship, and some years before he retired was named to the Board of the Nero First National Bank.

Lou and other Nero old-timers have followed with interest the story about the merger between the holding companies that con-

LOU LARRAWELL

trolled two upstate banks. An activist shareholder has brought pressure to bear on the merged bank to look around for an even bigger financial institution to scoop them up.

Lou Larrawell has a fear that — like his hardware store and the local funeral home just bought out by a national chain — Nero First National's days are numbered as a local institution, not to mention his own tenure on the Board. He has always enjoyed telling the daily gathering of grumps at the Arches that he can't stay late today and he is wearing his suit and tie because, well, you know, the Board of Directors meets later this morning. He enjoys sitting at the Board table and writing on the big, lined, yellow pads with the pens the bank provides. He'll admit it — being a director, having his picture on the board room wall, makes him feel important.

Lou is having regrets that he voted for the idea that Nero First National should go public. Lou doesn't know if any activist shareholders have purchased the bank holding company stock, which could hasten a takeover by some big bank from outside.

The truth is that it seems the best way to make money with a going business in a small city at the end of this American century is to sell out to a bigger concern.

Now that he's closed the hardware store, Lou might decide to finally move to Florida if some big bank comes in and he loses his seat on the First National board. Lou wouldn't be the first person to leave Nero because he had nothing more to do there, nor will he be the last.

❧

Pillar of Nero Society Pilloried for Being a Do-gooder
Whatever the question, the answer is no

In Nero, any new idea is greeted with distrust and skepticism. Whatever the question, the answer is no.

Nero-ites have many reasons why something shouldn't happen in their city. How could such a thing work in this forsaken place? Who is trying to do this? Will they get some benefit from it the rest of us will not? When our people came here we never got the breaks these new immigrants are getting — this could be a scheme to help them! If we try this project and fail, won't we be a laughingstock? It is a vicious circle.

To be fair, the negative attitude in Nero stems from the fact that the city has had its share of foolish schemes and connivers. Developers and industry have come and gone, taking the tax breaks and leaving the people to fend for themselves.

It is hard even for the pure of heart to build faith in the city's future, as a well-heeled and good-natured man recently learned.

Lou Larrawell, the retired proprietor of a now-defunct downtown hardware store, had hoped to create a Winter Carnival in Nero this year. Lou enjoys seeing his name in the paper and was hoping for a certain amount of praise for his good works. But believe it or not, and many townspeople did not believe it, Lou was mainly motivated by civic duty and a desire to give Nero-ites something to do in the cold, drab winter.

Lou is part of Nero's small but significant upper crust but he remembers his roots. When Lou was young, his family lived in a rundown flat with a gas space heater that gave intermittent heat during the cold winter nights.

Lou thought that a three-day carnival with ice sculpture contests, snowmobile races, Miss Winter Carnival competition, Snowflake Ball, free hot chocolate and the like would help make Nero more bearable in the winter. He was willing to foot part of the bill and hoped to get a few other people of means involved in supporting the effort.

One thing about Nero is that people don't damn new ideas with faint praise. People out and out trashed Lou's "harebrained and cockeyed plot."

The Nero city council member with the local political franchise on vitriol called Lou devious, a rich man out to make a profit from this Winter Carnival. "Where is this hot chocolate coming from? It's a money-making scheme," the council member told Mike on Mike's talk show on WNRO radio.

"Lou Larrawell is a fat cat who just doesn't get it," shouted Van Wilson during the next day's promotional announcement for the talk show, "The Never Ending Argument."

There were three vicious letters to the editor in the *Nero Nation* wondering what it was that conniving Lou Larrawell had up his sleeve, proposing a Winter Carnival and a beauty contest. One of the letter writers made a comparison between President Clinton's Monica Lewinsky troubles and Lou Larrawell's desire to assemble Nero's admittedly good-looking young women in one place for a beauty contest.

Lou gave up on the Winter Carnival and is giving more thought to relocating to Florida or some sunnier clime, although he remains a Nero booster at heart.

"I was only trying to do something good," he told his cronies at their morning gab session at the Golden Arches.

"Forget it," said one of his buddies. "Nobody in this town is willing to try anything new. Even the Chamber of Commerce doesn't boost Nero. They simply tell people the city isn't as bad as its reputation."

≥●

A Nero Upbringing Can Mean Success Elsewhere
A Nero native has had excellent survival training

One of the great ironies about Nero is that the city's native sons and daughters do very well when they seek their fortunes in the outside world.

Every so often the *Nero Nation,* the local paper, does a where-are they-now story about the immigrant kid from Nero who went on to be a major star in Hollywood, the local basketball standout who is a coach in the NBA, the high school football star who is now an investment banker or the former local tough who is a top-ranking officer in the military. Nero natives are successful doctors, lawyers, teachers, performers, politicians, technology masters and captains of industry in other parts of the country.

Wanda Tamburino, the office manager and constituent problem-fixer for Nero's popular Congressman, contended that growing up in Nero prepares people for success anywhere else in the country where there are more opportunities than in the declining home town.

"Whatever little bit you get here, you have to fight for," she maintained, when we ran into each other at Nero's struggling down-town chain hotel during Saturday lunch. "People here are good-hearted in a way but they are so frugal and stubborn that they don't give each other much help in business. With all the people I've helped during the years, you would think I'd have it made if I went into business around here. But I wouldn't count on it. Nero people might pull a drowning woman from the creek but she'd be on her own once they got her to shore."

The problems of the downtown hotel are a case in point. Three separate chains have tried to make a go of the hotel, an admittedly out-of-place, modernistic building, plunked downtown with the help of government financing during the free-spending days of 1970s urban renewal.

You might think that local people would patronize the hotel restaurant and try to help the current operator keep the struggling enterprise going, instead of hastening the poured concrete building's addition to Nero's growing portfolio of vacant, boarded-up structures.

The hotel lunch specials on Saturday included chicken tenders, honey mustard sauce and cole slaw for $3.95. For $4.95 you could get toasted turkey and cheese, with fries and a pickle. These are good prices for a hotel restaurant where the floor is regularly vacuumed, the furniture dusted, the plates and silverware clean and the wait staff attentive. The crowd, however, was slim.

In Nero, even $3.95 for lunch is at the upper end of the "can't-go-wrong-at-this-price" scale. Nero folks would rather frequent places where the luncheon bill is closer to $2.99, even if the floor in the cheaper place only sees a mop every so often, the outside walls cry out for a can of paint and the luncheon silverware bears traces of breakfast eggs.

Wanda told me: "A Nero native has had excellent survival training. He or she can usually run right over some poor soul from a richer part of the world. People in Nero argue over things that make no difference outside this environment. Growing up here is good training for success somewhere else."

Sometimes you wonder if one of the wildly successful natives will feel sorry for the home town, come back and invest some money to improve things. I believe a successful country singer did that for her home town in the south.

Wanda doubted that this would happen and she's probably right. Nero is the place that people leave if they can and live in only if they have to. First off, somebody who left Nero and made a fortune would not likely throw money away on such a sentimental project. Even if the Hollywood star, for example, started pumping money into the old hometown, Nero people would be skeptical, frugal and a bit standoffish. They would speculate and agonize over what the movie star's real motive could be in spending money in Nero. Of course, they'd cash whatever of his checks they could. Probably, they would not go too far out of their way to help him succeed.

⁂

Women Were the Glue in the Upstate Mill Towns
By Ruth Peterson, a contributor to the Sunday Gazette

Bob Cudmore, the scribe who narrates events in the declining, upstate city of Nero, describes a malaise of negativism gripping the place. Nefarious mill owners, unscrupulous politicians and citizens fearful of exploitation seem bent on destroying this idyllic spot.

Meanwhile, nearby in the very heart of Milltown, the lives of the wives of blue- and white-collar workers have gone largely unrecorded. I would like to think about the tools they used in their everyday lives and mention the social dynamics at play in Milltown.

In bygone days, the mill worker walked proudly off to work carrying his lunch bucket prepared earlier by his wife as she cooked his breakfast. It typically contained a pastrami, cheese or tuna fish sandwich, a huge dill pickle and flakey tarts or homemade cookies, all carefully wrapped in waxed paper. A large thermos of hot coffee fit neatly in the lid of the bucket.

If the breadwinner was one of the mill's managers, he might go home for lunch, or he might have had lunch at the Iroquois Inn, where sedate surroundings and fine food contributed to the sense of bonhomie necessary to transact business and entertain clients. This male bastion was also a fine place to stop in for a drink at the end of the day, when lesser workingmen might be dropping in their favorite pubs for a pint or two. Milltown wives were busy at home preparing the evening meal.

The needs of their husband and children were paramount to Milltown women, who spent their days in Northtown or up the hill in Overlook or in the quiet leafy glade known as Milltown Mansions. The status of her husband dictated what she did with her time. Much camaraderie existed over the back fences of first- and second-generation immigrant families in Northtown and Overlook — the exchanging of recipes, health tips, child-care advice mixed with friendly gossip. Other than this rich backfence life, neighborhood churches provided most of her social activity. Baptisms, confirmations, first communions, weddings and funerals punctuated her life. A well-fed husband, a spotless house and clean children provided her status.

On washday, women busied themselves with corrugated metal washboards, washtubs (later the new wringer washers) and clotheslines strung in the yard or from an upstairs window. Washday involved sorting the white and colored clothing — separately wringing them out, boiling and applying the starch and bluing, and hanging successive loads of wash outside. When dry, shirts, dresses and linens were dampened again for ironing. Before the advent of the electric iron, heavy flatirons were heated on the stove and used in rotation.

Some wives made their own soap from wood ashes and lye. If there was a baby in the house, cloth diapers had to be scrubbed, boiled and hung to dry. If baby formula was called for, it had to be mixed, poured into clean baby bottles with rubber nipples and boiled. Pity the poor Milltown housewife who went to bed without an adequate supply of formula to see her through the night.

Then there was the matter of window and floor coverings. Depending on neighborhood and custom, window treatment might include white sheers, lace curtains, heavy winter drapes and lighter summer curtains — often made at home. The good housewife used curtain stretchers for her sheer and lace curtains — a rectangular standing device with pins all the way around on which she stretched her curtains to the appropriate size. Heavy drapes were hung on the line and beaten. Cotton drapes were washed, starched, ironed and rehung.

Floors demanded a great deal of the Milltown wife's time. Wood floors had to mopped, oiled or waxed. Linoleum floors in kitchens and sometimes throughout the house demanded scrubbing on hands and knees with a scrub brush and a pail of hot, sudsy water. Then they were waxed and buffed. If the family prospered, carpets were added and had to be cleaned either with a stiff broom, or taken outside on a line and beaten with a metal rug beater — or at a later date, vacuumed with the new Hoover vacuum cleaner.

Many wives had large vegetable gardens, fruit trees and grapevines. As vegetables ripened, she brought her huge canner up from the cellar. This was fitted with a circular wire mesh rack to hold the jars and handles to lift the steaming contents from the hot water. First, she washed the jars, lids, and rings, and then prepared the beans, tomatoes, peas, corn, carrots, beets, squash and pumpkins for canning. She also might make pickles, relish, tomato juice, chili sauce, spaghetti sauce, and jams, jellies, chutney and conserve.

In the fall, she made applesauce, apple butter and cider. She might also buy peaches and pears by the bushel to can. Basement shelves were loaded with her handiwork. When the grapes ripened, in addition to making jelly, she might help her husband in the making of wine. Other women gathered dandelions from open fields to use in dandelion wine.

What of the women whose husbands rose to higher levels of management and who lived in Milltown Mansions? Her work was less physically demanding because her husband could afford household help — perhaps a housekeeper, a maid, dressmaker, cleaning woman, even a yard man. But there were exacting demands placed upon her, too. Her appearance was important, so she had to acquire a tasteful wardrobe. She was expected to entertain, and here she could display her gift for creating comfort and beauty with perfectly appointed linens, glassware, china flower arrangements and food impeccably prepared and served. Her social graces were put to use choosing and seating guests appropriately, introducing table conversation and providing an atmosphere that reflected well on her husband and his status at the mill.

With few exceptions, she didn't work outside the home or display her talents in other public ways, although she might be highly educated. She was encouraged to join her peers in book clubs, garden clubs, bridge clubs, music clubs and Milltown wives' clubs. In furthering their husbands' careers, most could have signed an oath to the mill similar to the Boy Scout Oath, with particular attention to "loyal."

Like their husbands, Milltown wives could be ambitious, lazy, brave, timid, kind, cruel, modest or self-serving. Would the mills have prospered without the wives of Northtown, Overlook and Milltown Mansions? Maybe, but without the domestic comforts provided by women. It might have more closely resembled the gold rush and logging camps of the Wild West.

New York Times Religion writer Peter Steinfels claims "Social, communal and moral resources hold a society together and make it productive." I would propose that the Milltown women provided many of the resources that contributed to the health and welfare of this once prosperous giant.

ન્ટ

Women's Work in Nero
Assigning blame is an ongoing process

A ssigning blame is an ongoing process in Nero. Some blame the unions for a long strike decades ago which preceded the wholesale departure of the sock industry to warmer climes. Others blame the industrialists who were lured south by cheap labor and tax breaks.

Oldtimers blame the new immigrants for current problems with crime, drugs and welfare dependency. Newcomers blame the old guard for refusing to give up any significant piece of the old order.

Determining fault is so ingrained that one of the greatest compliments in Nero is the following choice of words — "I don't blame you."

Occasionally, "I don't blame you" justifies having fun. If you have a few drinks after either getting promoted or fired, skip work and go to the track when Fourstar Dave is in attendance, or let the lawn go long and sleep in a hammock on a summer afternoon, a friend of yours — if not your spouse — might say "I don't blame you." There are limits, of course, and Nero-ites know that continued pursuit of good times can result in condemnation.

You are most properly told "I don't blame you" when it's obvious you've come to the end of your rope and, although what you are doing may not be pleasant or kind, you are doing what you have to do. You would say "I don't blame you" to a woman leaving her abusive husband or a hard-pressed family filing for a tax abatement.

If you had been at happy hour at the Four Clover Tavern in Nero last week, you would have heard Wanda Tamburino bestow an "I don't blame you," in absentia, on *Gazette* contributor Ruth Peterson for Ms. Peterson's column praising the hard work and civilizing influences that women have brought to upstate New York's mill towns.

"You dwell on the nefarious, unscrupulous and the fearful," Wanda said, referring to me and quoting Ms. Peterson. "Based on my experiences I can't blame you either, although you should write about women more often."

Well-connected in two ethnic communities, Wanda is the constituent problem-fixer for Nero's popular Congressman and knows Nero's negativity at first hand. She has heard many tales of woe, some of which are even true.

Ms. Peterson's account of the lunch-making, clothes-washing, stay-at-home women whose husbands worked in the mills was right on the mark, according to Wanda.

WANDA TAMBURINO

Wanda said: "Sometimes, it was a race to see whether the local tavern owner or housewife would get the week's paycheck in the old days. My grandfather was a hard-working soul, never missed a day of work in his life. Every Friday he took a good part of his pay and went out to get a pack of cigarettes and a beer. We didn't see him again until Sunday, when he returned with cuts and bruises from his weekend jaunt.

"In terms of the contributions of women in Nero, keep in mind that many women worked in the mills and even claimed their own seats at the taverns after work. Women are better at many factory tasks, if you ask me, and the mill owners must have thought the same thing because they hired quite a few women, usually paying them less than the men.

"I had a job in a clothing factory right out of high school. This mill was one of those sweatshops that came to Nero after the sock industry went south. One night, while staring at the work as it went by on my machine, I fell asleep. My job was to watch fabric being made, looking for any imperfections that would mean I'd have to stop the equipment. It wasn't rocket science but it was exacting, tedious and draining. The machine made an awful noise. Working in that sweatshop was like being hypnotized in hell.

"When I woke up, I had no idea if the fabric which had gone by was good, bad or indifferent. Maybe a guy would have let it go but I told the foreman. They docked my pay.

"That night, I decided to go to college and get a different kind of job. My mother wasn't pleased. The women in my family had always raised kids, worked in the mills or both. It was my older sister, who worked the night shift in a squirt gun factory while raising her family, who said she couldn't blame me. There are some things

I don't like about my current job but I'm sure that leaving that mill when I did was the best decision I ever made."

❧

If You Tear It Down, Will They Come?
A Nero fire attracts the gawkers

There is usually a bad fire each winter in Nero that provides copy for the local paper and creates a temporary tourist attraction. In February of this year, a terrible blaze took several lives and one more street gained a hole where a house used to be.

For weeks after the fire, an impromptu parade of cars slowly passed the burned-out building and the makeshift memorials in the snow and ice. Some motorists tried to make it seem as if they were simply driving from here to there as they gawked at the fire scene. Truthfully, few people normally travel that street, which contains one remaining business and about a dozen houses, two or three of them with "For Sale by Owner" signs. It is not the worst neighborhood in the city, although it is not the best neighborhood either.

Winter is not a pretty season in Nero, even on streets that have not had a fire. Ugly banks of dirty snow line the main streets. Even downtown sidewalks have stretches of ice long after the snow has been cleared from the roads because so many homes and businesses are abandoned.

But the sun shone brilliantly in early February, lifting the spirits of the residents, even those who were saddened by the losses from the fire. The bright sunlight was a wonderful tonic in the midst of the drab upstate winter. It made success seem attainable, and Nero's

MIKE VAN WILSON

people, at least momentarily, felt spring's optimism in their hearts.

Maybe that's why people in Nero read with interest the news stories about the plan to tear down homes near Schenectady's State Street to attract an industrial park to the Electric City.

Some Nero-ites are ready to support this concept for their own city, the former sock-making capital of the world, where so many people are on one form of government aid or another that some think Nero should be renamed Government Check.

"If tearing down houses to attract industry can be considered in Schenectady, why not here," one caller told talk host Mike Van Wilson on Mike's WNRO program, "The Never Ending Argument." "Just tear down that whole neighborhood where the fire was, move the people somewhere else, get a factory built and we'll be ahead of the game."

"I'm outraged you think that," countered Mike. "Next thing you know you'll be forgiving the President with the rest of the people in this loony country. Why should we tear down any more buildings in Nero? We already lose a bunch of buildings to ordinary fires every year and once in awhile some big blaze knocks out half an acre or something."

"But Mike, these holes around town are too scattered," the caller replied. "What we need is to get rid of three, four or five blocks of these down-and-out houses to attract some industry, get us some jobs."

Mike shot back: "Are you saying we don't have enough empty lots in one place in this falling down city? You are out of your mind!"

He shouted the last two sentences, knowing that sound bite would make a good promotional announcement for the next day's show.

Mike makes sense here, although I usually don't go along with his angrily voiced right-wing opinions, especially all the terrible things he has said about the President.

In this case, as Mike pointed out, empty lots and empty factory buildings litter the landscape in Nero. There is a 1960s era industrial park right outside town that is only one-quarter occupied.

I don't know about Schenectady, but Nero's problem does not appear to be a lack of space in the city for industry, but a lack of industry for the city's available space.

❧

Native Sons Can Be Mean
By B. John Jablonski

(B. John Jablonski, a columnist for The Recorder of Amsterdam, was greatly offended by the article If You Tear It Down, They Will Come. Here is his rebuttal to the negativity of Nero.)

Perhaps I am reading too much into it, or again, I may simply be putting the wrong spin on it. Nevertheless, I was deeply disturbed after reading it. The it I refer to, is an article in the opinion section, of an out-of-town newspaper. The piece refers to Nero, a mythical mill town in upstate New York.

The writing, in a veiled way, is a portrait of our city of Amsterdam. Other than belaboring the theme that our once bustling industries have left us, and we are a town of citizens with our hands out waiting for the dole, not much else is said. The flippant attitude of the narrative is what bothers me. If this composition had been written by some stranger, it would not cut as deeply. But, on the contrary, it was written by a native son. The ache is more acute because of this. Describing this supposedly mythical town is the statement, "In a regular Nero midwinter ritual, an impromptu parade of cars passed by the burnt-out building and makeshift memorials." It seems to me, as if the writer thinks it odd that people would want to see and show respect at the scene where a catastrophe had occurred. Isn't this done in every town that suffers a tragic loss? Is it necessary to describe these sympathizers as gawkers? Why not mention the heroic efforts of the fire department that contained the inferno to a minimum of damage?

The story goes on to say, "The former sock-making capital of the world, where so many people are on one form of government aid or another that some think Nero should be renamed, Government Check." This is the lowest degrading remark of all — a slap in the face to a town that is utilizing all means possible to maintain a safe and friendly environment for its elderly and young. Are not taxes sent to the seats of government by our citizens as well as those from other localities? Are we not entitled to receive at least a portion of this back as aid when it is needed?

The affluent, who have used and milked our city till there was little left to pick over, have gone on to greener pastures. So has the author of the story I refer to. It has been left to the citizens remaining here, to rebuild a new community from the residue.

As a former native son who now roams the more verdant pastures, the essayist no longer remembers the benefits he received from his neighbors. He forgets those who gave of themselves and their time so he, as a young lad, would have the benefits of various activities to broaden his mind. There is no mention of the ones who taught him the skills necessary to be successful in life. No acknowledgment to mentors who nurtured his career in broadcasting at our small town radio station. He does not live here anymore.

He can only bring it to mind in a disparaging mythical story of Nero. It would appear that he sees Amsterdam as a town of abandoned homes and businesses where, in his words, "Busy sidewalks have long stretches of ice long after the snow has been cleared from the roads." There was no mention of the projects aimed at revitalizing East Main Street. Where is the mention of the new immigrants to our city who settle here and take menial jobs at low wages just for the opportunity to become a part of it? These start out in the low cost areas of town and build their futures from there. His research did not dig deep enough to give credit to our police department and their diligent efforts to keep the city a safe place to live and raise a family.

The columnist did not turn the page in the same paper, the same day his commentary appeared, to read where Erin M. Harzinski, the city of Amsterdam's Community Development and Grants Assistant, stated that, "Expanding an already successful industrial park makes sense." This was included in a near full page story describing how the industrial park is challenged to make additional room for businesses investigating the possibilities of setting up shop in the area.

His description of the park states, "There is a 1960s era industrial park right outside town that is only one quarter occupied." There was no mention that in reality the park will have to hang out a No Vacancy sign next month because all existing structures are filled to capacity. Any recognition to our city planners for their efforts and success in filling the park, was nowhere to be found in his tale of Nero.

I personally am an adopted son of our town. I was first introduced to the area in 1948. I have lived here in years of plenty, and suffered with the rest of the citizenry in times of want. I have built my home here, have raised my family here, and someday will be laid to rest here. I do not dream of having lived my life differently, or wishing to have been elsewhere.

I've witnessed the arrogance of many as they spoke of our tired old mill town. However, I have seen and admired what others may have missed — the resolve of our people to pick themselves up time after time, dust themselves off, and begin rebuilding all over again. These are the people I write of with enthusiasm — those with faith, courage, and optimism. Call me a Pollyanna if you must, but the things I mention lead to success and the achievement of goals. Not giving voice to this, is a dereliction of duty.

A native son attempting to impress others with his mythical story of despondency, accentuating the negative and little or nothing of the positive, make the story disheartening to read and an injustice to our community. Cheap shots may be expected from strangers, but like Julius Caesar, I can only say, "Et tu, Bob Cudmore?"

&.

Nothing Good Ever Happens in Nero
Is Nero Amsterdam?

People in Nero feel they have finally hit bottom. And, unfortunately, it's my fault. "You've stripped us of our identity," my friend Disease Cotter told me last Saturday morning as he sipped a beer at Nero's Four Clover Tavern. I was having a coffee, honest to goodness, although, it being Saturday, the Four Clover was not serving lunch, just catering to the drinking crowd.

"I don't blame the men who wrote to the newspapers, I blame you," Disease said, referring to a recent letter to the *Gazette* from Lewis Carosella and a column in another local paper, both of which came to the conclusion that Nero is really Amsterdam, my home town.

"The letter writer says you 'don't have to be Sherlock Holmes' to know that Nero is Amsterdam," Disease spit out sarcastically, relishing the chance to watch me wince. "What an outrage. Nero is Nero. Do we have a riverfront park project underway in Nero as they do in Amsterdam?"

I didn't know what to say.

"No, we don't," said Disease, warming to his subject as he exercised the time-honored Nero custom of blamestorming. "We don't even have a river — we have a creek. And we don't have a successful industrial park in Nero, as they do in Amsterdam. We don't have two excellent hospitals. We don't have a school system that is advanced in today's technology. We don't have excellent recreational facilities. We don't even have a First Night! I spent New Year's Eve right here at the Four Clover. You should know, my literary friend, you wrote about it. How is it that you have made people assume from your stupid little stories about our city that you are really writing about Amsterdam?"

I didn't know what to say.

By then, radio personality Mike Van Wilson was blaring from the radio in the Four Clover with his WNRO talk show and he, too, was on my case: "As if this falling down city doesn't have enough trouble, here this writer and self-professed liberal is spinning stories about Nero so twisted and distorted that some people think he's talking about Amsterdam."

Mike continued: "If Amsterdam is really Nero, we are all in trouble. In Amsterdam, there is hope. Of course, Amsterdam is something like Nero. Every town in upstate New York has something in common with Nero — with the possible exceptions of chic Saratoga Springs, suburban Clifton Park or maybe tax-less Wilton with all those businesses clogging the Northway trying to move in. Sure, Nero is like Amsterdam, but Nero is also like Cohoes, Hudson, Ilion, Utica, Troy, Johnstown, Schenectady, you name it. The point is that our city is the worst. Nothing good ever happens in Nero. It's as simple as that. I'd give my right arm to work in radio in Amsterdam. Heck, they have more than one station in the former Rug City and one of them even plays classical, highbrow music. You couldn't get away with that in Nero — the city to leave if you can and live in only if you have to!"

Mike shouted the last sentence, realizing it would make a good sound bite to promote Monday's program.

On the way out of Nero, I passed the scruffy little Nero Aerodrome that will never be named an international airport. Like the big International Airport in Albany, though, the Nero Aerodrome doesn't have very many international flights, but that's another story.

Looking at the worn-out hanger, the small cluster of little planes and the bumpy runway, I knew I'd failed the people of Nero.

They take a perverse pride in being the worst place in Upstate New York. Their negativity, their being down-at-the-mouth, is about all they have left. With people mistaking Nero for Amsterdam, Nero's residents feel they have lost their identity.

ಶ

The Sporting Life

Surely sports are more important than most things in life

L ast week's spring downpour came close to engulfing what's left of downtown Nero. Billows of spray rose from the Keepthemunda Creek, like the spray you see when you are still miles away from Niagara Falls.

At midday, the flooding provided an excuse for regulars to have a beer at the Four Clover Tavern, where the parking lot has a good view of the raging creek. Just to be safe, the bartender took down the valuable pictures of the Nero High School basketball team and kept them in the trunk of his car for the day. Aside from flooding a few streets, though, the rising waters did no real damage to the Four Clover, the other old store buildings, and abandoned mills in downtown Nero.

The flood made Nero-ites momentarily forget their obsession with the story of the Fonda-Fultonville football players, accused in the "bottle bomb" incident. Nero-ites understand why so many people in Fonda-Fultonville take the side of the coach who let the accused players back on the field after a short suspension.

Nothing good has happened for a long time in Nero, except that the high school basketball team, the Nero Fiddlers, made it to the sectionals last season. The boys on the team became local heroes. The men in Nero had something to brag about. A glimmer of hope could be felt even in those ramshackle mobile homes on the edge of town that have Aspenite covering some of the windows and broken all-terrain vehicles littering the yard. Nero was finally known for something exciting, it was no longer simply another "armpit of the nation."

For some of the boys on the team, maybe for most of them, few things in their lives will bring the attention that they reap from high school basketball. All this attention makes some of the boys feel they are better than everyone else.

Nero Police had a tough situation on their hands when the star player on the basketball team beat up his girlfriend the weekend before the sectionals. The girl was hospitalized but did live. The boy was not suspended from the team. The incident had not happened on school time nor on school property. The player had to sit out one practice. The Nero Fiddlers won the sectional game and any moral error was eclipsed by the momentary erasure of the drabness and poverty of life in Nero because of this victory.

Surely, sports are more important than most things in life. Some people lament that sports excellence gets more attention than academics. Well, every newspaper has a sports section. Show me a newspaper with an academics section. There is a nightly sports report on television, but no nightly television report on morality. Without a successful high school sports program, Nero would be more depressing than it is.

Still, some in Nero feel that something is wrong. The Nero basketball player who beat his girlfriend got to play in his big game and will probably end up on probation. Conscientious Nero-ites compare that young man's fate with a black youth from Albany who went to jail for nine to eleven years for taking a gun to school. It may not be only a racial thing. If the Albany youth had been a sports star, he might have fared better.

After the sectional victory, the Nero Fiddlers lost the state basketball semi-finals to a powerful downstate team. "Wait until next year," is what folks in Nero say. The good people of Nero are hoping that next year they will finally be able to erect a sign on the state highway that says: "Nero, home of the Nero Fiddlers Boys' Basketball Team, State Champions."

Winning may not be everything. But if the high school basketball team can produce a state trophy, there is little doubt that most people in Nero will be willing to excuse more unseemly conduct by the players.

❧

A Depressing City

"Used to be" is a favorite phrase in Nero

When Disease Cotter heard about the latest GE cutbacks in Schenectady, it got him thinking about the economic history of Nero, which used to be the sock-making capital of the world.

"Used to be," said Disease, "is a favorite phrase in Nero. 'That used to be Sock Mill Number One,' someone might say. 'Used to be a tavern there that the guys on the third shift went to at 8 in the morning,' someone else will remark."

The problems they're having in Schenectady Nero had decades

ago. The sock mills moved south in the sixties and years later went offshore.

A whole generation of Nero-ites has grown up in a depressed area. The local business people tried to get new industry. What were attracted were companies that paid less than the sock mills did. And the sock mills never paid like GE.

Then these new companies had problems. One of the companies made a phone-answering machine that was about as useful as a doorstop and that company folded. Another company made squirt guns but lost the patent to the Super Soaker and had to close up shop.

Nero city officials tore down a good part of downtown, which had become an eyesore. But what was put in was one of those undesirable, one-quarter used, intown malls.

The new immigrants and the old immigrants are at odds. The new people don't have many places to work and some are on welfare. Some of the older people are on welfare, too, because of the cost of health aides in the home or being in a nursing home.

Cheerfulness is not a common emotion in Nero. Oh sure, people can be happy when going to a sporting event, betting on the horses at OTB or having a few beers at the taverns. But a positive attitude is pretty rare.

Living in a depressed area does a number on your self-esteem. Even things that seem to happen for the good in Nero always have a down side.

They're finally putting up some big stores on the north side of the city but all the people are doing is fighting over the project and predicting problems when the stores open. There's going to be too much traffic, some say. Politicians argue whether the new buildings are too close to the road or whether the city should give the stores fire protection, even though the buildings are just outside the city.

No one in Nero believes that anything good can happen here. The people are always talking about luck or, really, the lack of luck.

"With my luck I'll go to one of those new stores and get hit by a truck."

"With our luck as soon as we have a big rainstorm that new parking lot will cause a flood in what's left of this crummy city."

"With your luck if you get a job at that place it'll be out of business by Christmas."

Then, true to form, some bone-headed decision is uncovered which confirms everyone's suspicion that Nero is cursed. In the case of the new stores it turns out that they've built one of them on a swamp. Nobody can figure how to keep the water off the sales floor. As always, this gets a lot of attention from the news media (NEW NERO STORE ALL WET) and it's one more nail in the coffin of Nero's self-image.

ॐ

It Never Fails

Life goes on in Nero

It never fails. Whenever you decide to do something, it's the wrong time. When you give up waiting for a call and head for the bathroom, the phone rings. When you schedule a vacation out of town, you get an invitation to your cousin's wedding for that very weekend. When you decide to visit the new fast-food outlet in Nero, the whole city gets the same idea.

My friend Disease Cotter and I went to the new Wendy's in Nero last Saturday. Coincidentally, a new Wendy's recently opened in the more prosperous Amsterdam area.

The Wendy's parking lot was full, although we got a spot using Disease's handicapped tag. Disease knows people at City Hall and, honestly, he's still bothered by his childhood condition — which is why he's called Disease — and he strained his back shoveling snow into the street during the last winter storm.

Why we didn't have the sense to give up in the crowded parking lot is a mystery. When we got into the slow-moving line inside, Disease said that it would have been a good day to visit Joe's Kitchen — Nero's traditional greasy spoon — or even the Golden Arches.

The grumpy old men's club from the Golden Arches had deserted their traditional morning spot to try Wendy's. They were ahead of us in line, along with a horde of hungry teens, a nuclear family or two, some grandparents and grandchildren and single mothers with their kids.

The sun was shining and Nero looked optimistic, like America should, even though the tables were small, bombs were falling in Serbia, the line was long, the state budget was late and the restaurant was running out of a few things.

"Why did we come here today when we knew there would be such a crowd?" Disease mused. He proceeded to answer his own question, while providing commentary on the food.

"We want to get it over with, for one thing. In Upstate New York, even people who are late are early. We can't stand the idea that we missed out on something. Is this Frosty thing a milkshake or a Sundae? I blame the mills for everybody pouncing on anything new. I always wanted to work first shift, get it over with, take a nap and then get up for dinner and some TV. Do they have any butter for these baked potatoes? I don't like sour cream. Also, we always want to try someplace new, our options being limited in Nero. I enjoy the daily special at Joe's Kitchen, but there's just so much rice pudding you can eat in one lifetime. Did I order these onions on this hamburger? I didn't want onions.

"You could come back to this place in a month and it'll probably be so empty you could bowl down the center aisle. Could these tables be any smaller or is it that we're so big? Another thing, we're afraid of missing out on something free in Nero. I haven't seen them give anything away here, but I'm looking. This hamburger is actually pretty good. We're always hoping for free stuff. You know, this coffee is all right.

"You need the right attitude, though. My father, for example, was too honest. He was the first civilian on the scene when a tractor trailer spilled its load on the highway once, all kinds of stuff all over the place. He took a couple of pocket combs that fell out of a box and felt guilty. Next day, he was talking with his buddies at the mill. They came on the wreck later than he did and took boxes of combs, canned goods and even some small appliances.

"It never fails. The first guy on the scene of a bonanza of free stuff and it's my honest father. Let me put some of these creamers in my shirt and then we're out of here. Give me some sugars, too."

ॐ

Life In a Northern Town

Our most endearing trait is
how we still take care of each other

The 1995 movie "Nobody's Fool," starring Paul Newman, put our kind of upstate New York on the motion picture map. The movie is based on a novel by Gloversville native Richard Russo. You can tell that Russo has lived around here. Famed theatrical designer Joseph Aulisi, an Amsterdam native, did the costumes — maybe from memory.

People in Ballston Spa suspect the movie's fictional setting of North Bath is meant to be Ballston Spa. The movie's scenes were shot in the Hudson Valley: Fishkill, Beacon, Hudson and Poughkeepsie.

"It was hard to tell where the crowd at the Cinema Four in Nero left off and the movie began," said Disease Cotter when he and I met for a shot and a beer at the Four Clover on the Saturday after he saw the movie. "People in that movie wore jackets I've worn, drank in bars and ate in diners like the ones I have frequented, and liked to gamble, just like I do. And how about all the buildings in the movie with asphalt siding! Asphalt siding, to cover a rotting interior with a new exterior that isn't even pretty, symbolizes Nero's problems. We can't discard the bad parts of the past — we just cover them up with something even uglier.

"One asphalt siding kind of scheme in the movie was the rich people trying to open a theme park that you knew had odds of success worse than winning the trifecta. Every so often some idea like that comes along in Nero that somehow we're on the way back. It hasn't happened yet.

"My favorite character in the movie was the seedy and goofy construction guy Rub, partly because he has a funny nickname like me. The way Rub asked questions and hung on to the Paul Newman character reminded me of guys I've known. Old friends are a little strange, but they're the best.

"The movie made me appreciate some of the good things we have. Funny things happen here, like the nude poker game in the movie. You have to laugh, as the saying goes.

"We have lost jobs and hope in Nero. We sometimes forget that our most endearing trait is how we still take care of each other. Even if we play jokes on each other, insult each other and don't always like each other, we're usually ready to lend a hand.

"There's a saying in Nero that there's always a deal. You'll find mean people aplenty in Nero but there's usually somebody who will give you a break — like the Paul Newman character in 'Nobody's Fool' talking the old woman out of walking in slippers through the snow.

"Living in Nero can get you down sometimes. 'Nobody's Fool' made me realize that our way of life does have its nobility."

꙳

Nero Negativity Reflected In National Poll
Duci too optimistic for Nero politics

The negative mindset of Nero may be taking hold on a national scale. In fact, Nero's well-known negativity may be the real reason a popular Schenectady politician will choose not to run for mayor of Nero.

A 1999 poll found a new American pessimism linked to war in

Serbia and killings of high school students in Colorado. In Nero, the war touched off numerous arguments. No less an authority on modern warfare than the local newspaper, the *Nero Nation,* editorialized against the NATO bombing campaign as soon as it began for the campaign's lack of positive results.

The shootings in Colorado contributed to unease at Nero High School and even at the Keepthemunda Central High School in the prosperous suburbs, where teachers have been warily scanning their charges with their baggy pants, facial jewelry and backwards hats for signs of stress.

Nero's anxious mindset is now more typical of America, according to Washington-based pollster Celinda Lake. She told reporters that nine of ten participants in focus groups in various cities used words such as depressed, disappointed, anxious and confused to describe their assessment of the nation's present and future.

Nero, the former sock-making capital of the world, has been a depressed city for decades. It has been the scene of many disappointments, from the failed 1970s sock museum to the new big box stores that are built on swampland and prone to flooding.

Anxiety is a Nero birthright. Even when times are good, a person from Nero constantly worries that his own personal unlucky number is about to be announced by some celestial Bingo caller. No one in Nero believes that anything good will ever happen again.

Confusion, too, is commonplace in Nero, as evidenced by the old mill town saying, "I didn't know whether to laugh or cry," recently used by the movers and shakers when considering the suggestion that Schenectady's Frank Duci should run for mayor of Nero.

A Duci mayoral candidacy in Nero was suggested, perhaps facetiously, by Lewis Carosella in a recent letter to the *Daily Gazette.*

One of those exulting in the idea was *Nero Nation* columnist Don Leock, who wrote: "I say to the idea of a Duci candidacy in Nero, in the words of that great American George Herbert Walker Bush, LET'S GET IT ON!"

Nero's politicians were more sorrowful, knowing that Duci would campaign circles around any of them. However, wiser heads in the political camps eventually prevailed, making two important points.

Number one, Frank Duci would never abandon Schenectady to run for office in Nero. Duci's roots are in Schenectady, as are his friends and relatives.

Number two, Frank Duci is much too optimistic for the people of Nero.

"I remember when Frank wanted to bring the Emmys to Schenectady: that is an idea from an optimistic man," my old friend Disease Cotter said as we enjoyed a huge order of french toast at the recently refurbished Creek Diner, one of the first commercial beachheads of Nero's new immigrants. "Frank is too much the positive thinker to get enough votes to win a citywide election in Nero. Remember when he wanted to buy lottery tickets to help Schenectady? With our luck in Nero, we know that wouldn't work. As much as I would love to have the guy knocking on my door for votes, I think Frank Duci would do us all a favor if he ran for office in Schenectady where the people — except maybe some of the politicians in his own party — really appreciate him."

➤

Y2K Jitters Unsettle the Good People of Nero
Popular ice cream flavor is Y2K compliant

Radio talk host and computer expert Kim Komando attributes media fixation on computer problems disrupting life in the year 2000 to the idea that fear — along with greed and sex — are time-tested audience builders. At least for the media, fear can be good for business.

Franklin D. Roosevelt told Americans in 1933 that they had "nothing to fear except fear itself." That was a wise although partly disingenuous comment, given that many Americans then were fearful because of real poverty and real hunger.

Dread and anxiety have dominated the thinking of Nero residents since the Depression and the events that followed: war, deindustrialization and ongoing ethnic rivalries. In Nero, cheerfulness is not a common emotion, although the people always seem to get by.

"What I've been doing is putting aside twenty bucks each week in cash," said Disease Cotter, my old friend and retired Nero mill worker. "By the end of the year, I'll have maybe $500, that'll probably tide me over, unless my Social Security gets messed up."

Some older Nero residents routinely stash cash in secure home hiding places, a legacy of fear over bank failures in the Depression.

Disease discussed the Y2K dilemma while we enjoyed late summer of 1999 dishes of peach/pistachio ice cream at the Kreme 'n Kone just outside Nero, where owner Harvey Wadnobi makes his own ice cream. Remarkably, peach/pistachio is the house specialty.

"I'm stocking up on bottled water," Disease continued. "I buy it anyway, because the water here is so putrid. I figure I'll have 40 or 50 gallons stashed by the end of the year. I don't know why I like this peach/pistachio so much, it is a weird combination. I won't buy any ice cream at the end of the year, in case the power goes. But I'm getting in some peanut butter, saltines, canned stuff. Maybe two or three cans of gasoline for my generator. Hey Harvey, I hope your ice cream machine is Y2K compliant, I'd hate to be stuck without my peach/pistachio next summer."

"You bet my ice cream maker is Y2K compliant," Harvey shouted from the back room, with probably more real conviction than government and industry officials have been able to communicate on Y2K compliance.

Talk host Mike Van Wilson was sputtering now on his WNRO radio program, which we could hear on the old radio behind the counter at the Kreme 'n Kone.

"You people should make sure you and yours can get by on your own for a few days in the year 2000," Mike said, building into his customary screaming crescendo. "But this Y2K problem should be blamed on one man — the First Prevaricator, President-Two Faced, the philandering husband of the woman whose election to the U.S. Senate would set this state on the road to liberal lunacy. Where has Bill Clinton been for the past eight years as the clock has ticked closer and closer to the year 2000? You know where he's been and you know what he's been doing. When your power is off in January, when your blessed government checks don't come in the mail, remember to blame Bill Clinton and vote for George W. Bush!"

Although Mike's last statement would become the promotional announcement for the next show, several callers hijacked the program from Mike's anti-Clinton diatribe into a typically Nero-esque fixation on worrying about every imaginable calamity.

"People are going to be robbed," one caller said. "That's the real problem. People stashing money and food and generators and gasoline at home are going to be victimized. Mark my words, Mike, there's going to be a rash of burglaries before year 2000. The cops will have to do something about it. We'll have to spend our tax dollars protecting these hoarders."

In Nero, you're blamed if you do and blamed if you don't.

ૐ

Ignored By Gore

Top politicians avoid Nero

When Vice President Al Gore toured Amsterdam and Fulton County in a display of compassion for Upstate New York and an effort to garner votes for his presidential campaign, the movers and shakers in Nero responded, "Typical, we've been ignored again." In Nero, the better days ended when the sock mills closed shortly after the Eisenhower administration.

"Al Gore may be dull and, as Senator Moynihan says, he may be unelectable," wrote Don Lesock in a recent column in the *Nero Nation*. "However, Gore knows better than to waste his time with a trip to this armpit of the nation.

"Why didn't he come here? First, he couldn't find Nero. I don't blame him, most out-of-town politicians get lost on their way to this burg. Second, he couldn't pronounce or spell Keepthemunda. That would have made him a laughingstock on the talk shows. Third, he couldn't announce a federal grant here because our politicians can't agree on anything. We haven't come up with an idea for a federal grant since the days of LBJ when we got federal money to put up the stupid sock museum."

"Don's at it again, running down Nero in his column and making life tough for me and my boss" groused Wanda Tamburino, the constituent problem-fixer for Nero's popular Congressman as we met for a drink at the Four Clover Tavern. Wanda knows Nero's negativity first hand, having listened to many tales of woe, some of which are even true

"Of course, the Congressman tried to get the Vice President here," she continued. "We got the usual run-around about scheduling and demographics. We're out of step in Nero in terms of what politicians want. For Gore and for Hillary, even, we don't have enough soccer moms. We can't turn out those 30-something women with vans and SUVs who might be willing to vote if they think the candidate is going to spend more money on education. It's almost enough to make you want to become a Republican. But I don't think George W. Bush is going to come here, either. For example, can you imagine someone in Nero wanting to start a charter school?

"If we could have come up with some kind of announcement for the Vice President to make, he might have risked a trip to Nero. But it was typical. We couldn't get the locals to agree. I wanted to get a grant to rehab an abandoned mill for a community center. But the old guard was afraid it might help the new immigrants and 'who wants to help them,' they said. The mayor was for it, so the president of the city council was against it. Then, the paper found out my brother-in-law was in the running to be subcontractor for the air conditioning and that didn't look right. It's a small city, can I help it that my sister's husband makes has to make a living?"

Sometimes, Wanda pays a price for being well connected in two ethnic communities,

"I wish I lived in Amsterdam," Wanda said as she signaled Stan the bartender for another sombrero. "Even though they make their share of mistakes, people in Amsterdam keep trying new things — building a community center, putting up a museum, publishing a new paper, starting a band, even constructing that substantial foot-bridge that goes from the mall to the river for some reason.

"You have to hand it to hand it to the people in Amsterdam. They're still in the game. In Nero, we've thrown in the towel."

You Can't Go Wrong

Other Tales

You Can't Go Wrong

Designing Mohawk Carpets, Amsterdam, New York

ॐ

Casual Attire Unsettles this Male's Ego

Can dirty sneakers be worn on dress-down Friday?

Dress-down Friday scares the pants off me. In offices that allow the casual look on Fridays, men confront clothing choices previously faced only by women. This trend could do more to raise men's consciousness than all the relationship books on the best-seller list.

On dress-down Friday in the summer, should I put on the frayed short-sleeve shirt worn while cutting the lawn, along with the grass-stained sweat pants? How about the sneakers used to tar the driveway? Much to the chagrin of the women around me, no one has ever accused me of being dapper.

According to a fashion expert, on dress-down Friday a man could wear tailored pants with sport coat and casual shirt, shirt and vest, or woven shirt. Maybe he'd wear a suit in a sporty fabric. "Many men don't have a clue," New York City fashion forecaster Steve Gold admitted. Just call me clueless.

Younger men are more inclined to enjoy dressing casually at work, according to Gold, who pointed out that paunchy older men look better in tailored suits. Just call me paunchy.

My approach to dress is three-fold. I'm either not dressed, sort-of-dressed or dressed. My not-dressed look is more than casual or dress-down. There are the ink-stained chinos, superbly wrinkled blue shirt and the 20-year-old ripped and bedraggled parka.

Although I have the sense not to wear these clothes to work, my not-dressed look has been seen in public. "You wore those to church?" my wife has asked, repeating the old saw that women are blamed for the way the men look, even when men are on their own.

For dress-down Friday I affect my sort-of-dressed look — a sport coat that may be a touch big or small depending on the state of my diet, a shirt that may have the beginnings of a frayed neck, chinos and scuffed shoes. People usually see me when I'm at my desk, with the shoe-view conveniently blocked. My sort-of-dressed outfit usually could use some dry cleaning.

If it's a big day at work I go for the gold with my dressed look — a clean suit and tie, or a blazer with gray slacks and tie. I like to think left of center but dress like George Bush.

My ties, though, are colorful and sometimes outrageous. My closet boasts ties depicting Beatles songs, Norman Rockwell paintings, skyscrapers, cartoon characters and favorite objects, like hot dogs. Some are high fashion indeed, if you'll pardon the pun, designed by the late Jerry Garcia. Others sport splashy depictions of people and things drawn for good causes such as Save the Children or UNICEF. My wife buys them for me.

Going through a Saratoga receiving line years back, Mary Lou Whitney complimented me on one of my Beatles ties (Yellow Submarine, very colorful). When I tried to use tie-talk as a springboard to more conversation, she properly but forcefully pushed me along, but still, she noticed. Ties have been good to me. Some men complain about wearing ties. I don't.

Imagine my chagrin to learn that another development in the casual dress juggernaut is a move to eliminate the necktie. In a speech opening a show of African fashion, Prince Claus of the Netherlands removed his necktie and tossed it at the feet of his wife, Queen Beatrix. Calling the necktie "a snake around (his) neck," the 73-year-old prince received a standing ovation. A Dutch TV anchorman took off his tie while reporting the story and the station sports-caster followed suit. The anti-tie movement is now called "Claustrophilia." What next?

Could it be that the growing popularity of casual dress will affect the employability of the formally attired? A friend went on an interview at a firm with business casual attire Monday through Thursday (whatever that means) and dress-down day Friday.

My friend came dressed by the old rules, felt awkward and did not get the job. "I was a suit," he said.

❧

Check It Out

Are the lights off? Of course.

You've seen those surveys which show that in your lifetime you spend 25 years asleep, seven years at table, six months waiting in line and a month or two flossing your teeth. When the Big Guy does the final time study of my life, He'll find I spent years checking things.

When I parked my car the other morning and went to the office, I knew I had already turned off the lights. I turned off the lights before arriving at the parking lot. I always do. But as soon as I started walking from my car, carrying a briefcase and lunch bag and some newspapers, an internal debate began.

"Are the lights off?" ("Of course.") "But if the lights are on, we'll come back eight hours later to a dead battery." ("The lights are off.") "Look, it will take just a minute or two to go back to the car and check the lights. ("I'm late for work.") "Come on, if those lights are on, what a hassle. A jump start, a tow truck." ("Please, the lights are off.") "Sure?" ("Positive.") "Sure we're positive?" ("All right, let's check the lights.")

The lights were off, of course. Walking away from the car I started wondering if the dome light was still on. That dome light stays on if you don't shut the driver's door just so.

Psychologists say such behavior is only a problem when it really interferes with your life. You be the judge. The *Diagnostic and Statistical Manual of Mental Disorders of the American Psychiatric Association* calls the condition Obsessive-Compulsive Disorder. Those who suffer from it are said to have an Obsessive Compulsive Personality. TV talk shows have even added panels of obsessive-compulsives to their regular stable of people with sexual and relationship problems. Jack Nicholson played an obsessive-compulsive in the movies.

My particular little routine with the car lights seems to fit into the psychology manual description of compulsion: repetitive, purposeful and intentional behavior performed in response to some imagined or possible threat. On the plus side, employers often value obsessive-compulsives for their diligence.

"I wonder if I've sent this month's piece to *The Gazette*?" ("Of course.") "Sure?"

If I were mindful when I turned off the car lights or used the fax machine, as opposed to performing the task mindlessly, I would have a better chance remembering. *The New York Times* reported on Harvard psychologist Ellen J. Langer who studies *Mindfulness*, the title of her latest book. Much of the time, Langer says, we are on automatic pilot, not thinking about what we're doing. We forget things — misplacing car keys, going to the basement for something and forgetting why we went.

After studying the subject for many years, Langer concluded we can be taught to be more aware. She said that skills should be taught conditionally so that people learn to respond differently to changing situations.

Langer cited an example of mindlessness that may have happened to you. The professor was using a new credit card in a department store. The clerk saw that Langer had not signed the card and gave it to her to sign. When Langer then signed the receipt for the transaction, the clerk compared the signature on the receipt to the signature on the card to see if they matched. Duh.

Thinking of credit cards, though, did I mail a check to Master Card this month? ("Of course.") Am I sure?

❧

Whatever Happened to the Russian Lady?

If you worked in radio, this has happened to you

She was called the Russian Lady because of her noticeable Russian accent. A regular caller to Dick Taylor's 1970s era "Sound Off" talk show at WBEC radio in Pittsfield, Massachusetts, the Russian Lady was a joy. She didn't attack the host or the other callers and she always had some good point to contribute to the program.

The Russian Lady died. Dick Taylor saw the obituary, which even mentioned how the woman was known on radio as the Russian Lady. Dick did a tremendous tribute to her that day on his show and all the calls for several days on "Sound Off" dealt with what a wonderful person the Russian Lady had been.

Time went on and people stopped talking about the Russian Lady and started calling about fluoride in the water, the Trilateral Commission, the dog leash law — the hot topics of the day. A couple of weeks after the death of the Russian Lady a man called Dick's show and said: "Dick, there was a woman who used to call your program all the time, the Polish lady or the Ukrainian lady . . ." "You mean the Russian lady?" "Yeh, the Russian Lady, whatever happened to her?" Dick replied: "Sir, the Russian lady died a couple of weeks ago and we miss her very much." After that call, once again more calls came in praising the good qualities of the Russian Lady.

More time elapsed. Two months after the death of the Russian Lady, a woman called Dick's show and said: "Mr. Taylor, you used to have a regular caller named the Russian Lady. What's the matter, Mr. Taylor, did you offend her or cut her off or something? What gives, Mr. Taylor?" With admirable politeness, Dick replied: "Ma'am, I never did anything to offend the Russian Lady, but you see, she died two months ago." "Oh, I hadn't heard about that," the caller replied. Once again the whole program that day reverberated with praise of the Russian Lady.

Six months after the Russian Lady's death, out of nowhere, another call: "Dick, I think it's a damn' shame you don't let the Russian Lady call your talk show anymore. I believe another caller mentioned this some time back. We all liked the Russian Lady and, frankly, I'd rather listen to her common sense than listen to you pontificate." "Sir," said Dick Taylor through clenched teeth, "THE RUSSIAN LADY IS DEAD. SHE IS DEAD, DEAD, DEAD. SHE DIED SIX MONTHS AGO."

No matter how many times he explained it, the calls kept coming. A year later: "Dick, whatever happened to the Russian Lady?"

"SHE MET HER MAKER! SHE KICKED THE BUCKET! SHE BOUGHT THE FARM! SHE'S PUSHING UP DAISIES! SHE'S DEAD!!! WHAT MORE DO YOU PEOPLE WANT ME TO SAY ABOUT THIS?"

Dick Taylor is now the general manager of a radio station in Waterloo, Iowa. If you're ever in Iowa — and want to get a rise out of somebody — call his station, ask to speak to Mr. Taylor and when they ask you who is calling, simply say "the Russian Lady" and hang up.

There is a saying in the military — no matter how hard you try, somebody doesn't get the word.

≈

And Who the (Expletive Deleted) Are You?

Always leave them laughing

The late Henny Youngman (1906-1998) gamely kept us laughing through this vale of tears mainly for the joy it brought to him and the rest of us. (Youngman every day to the maitre d' at the Friars Club in Manhattan: I'd like a table near a waiter.) However, Youngman never let you forget that he made his living telling jokes. (Youngman: A fellow called up and said "What time is the next show?" I said: "What time can you make it?")

If Jerry Seinfeld has made nothing into comedy, Henny Youngman showed the importance of making everything a joke. (Youngman: I went to the doctor and he said: "I'm giving you six months to live." I said: "I demand a second opinion!" He said: "You're ugly.")

Walt Fritz, raconteur and former radio personality who now works at WRGB-TV, tells a Henny Youngman tale that is not a one-liner. Schenectady native and broadcast manager Lou Verruto was deputized some years ago to arrange Henny Youngman's appearance at a retirement party for a salesman at a TV station where Verruto then worked in New Haven, Connecticut. (Youngman: I won't say business was bad at the last place I played but the band was playing "Tea For One.")

Verruto, now the general manager of a TV station in Buffalo, didn't know how to reach Youngman but learned the comic had a listed phone in Manhattan, which he answered himself. (When the phone rang in his apartment, Youngman would sometimes say: "Answer it, it could be a job!" When the William Morris Theatrical Agency opened an office near Youngman's apartment, the comedian put a sign in his window that said: "Book thy neighbor.")

A deal was struck, Verruto was instructed to pick up Youngman in midtown Manhattan in a limousine for the ride to New Haven. Verruto thought the comedian would be accompanied by an entourage but at the appointed hour, Youngman was alone, clutching his violin case, waiting for his ride to New Haven. (Youngman: I just came from a pleasure trip. I took my mother-in-law to the airport.)

It was not an ordinary evening. (Youngman: A guy says to another guy: "Do you know the way to Central Park?" "No I don't." "That's OK, I'll mug you here.") After a Youngman-ordered stop at a deli for some corned-beef-sandwich refueling, Verruto emphasized to Youngman how much a fan the guest of honor/retiring salesman was. (Youngman: The food in that deli is fit for a king. Here, King.) Youngman tried out several lines for Verruto's benefit in the limo but saved the best for the party.

Entering the hall, the comic approached the star-struck guest of honor and said: "Who the (expletive) are you." It was the start of a memorable testimonial.

The world would be all but unbearable without the laughs. (A cartoon in the *New Yorker,* shows the Angel of Death confronting Henny Youngman. Youngman: Take my wife — please!)

ಿ

Going, Going, Gone
When you grow old, they take your stuff away

I t's not twilight time for the baby boomers but it certainly isn't morning in America any more. Veteran musician Al Kooper played a poignant song at a Van Dyck show in Schenectady called "Going, Going, Gone." The song mourned Kooper's inability to buy a new pair of the same kind of boots he'd been wearing for 15 years.

"They don't make 'em anymore, Al," he was told.

I like to wear sneakers with low soles, figuring I'm tall enough already and don't need high shoes to increase my clunkiness. The last thing I want to do in life is fall down.

However, noticing the growing popularity of big and high sneakers, will there come a day when the salesman will say, "Bob, they don't make low-soled sneakers anymore. They're as out-of-date as a one-speed bike, a push-button transmission or a personal computer without a mouse. Maybe you can find some of those old-fashioned sneakers at a garage sale with other relics like eight-track tapes, vinyl records and flash bulbs."

One of the founders of Blood, Sweat and Tears some 30 years

ago, song-writer Kooper also reported that the movie theater of his youth is gone, replaced by a drugstore, and that you no longer can buy an answering machine with a standard audio cassette.

When you grow old, they take your stuff away, Kooper concluded. Watching relatives age and, by choice or necessity, inhabit smaller and smaller spaces, I know that he is right. Some relatives did not go gentle into that good night, hating to part with old possessions as they moved from house, to apartment to nursing home room. On the other hand, some relished the idea of travelling lighter near the end of life's road.

Getting rid of personal things is not the same phenomenon as losing familiarity with the common objects and customs around you.

It's a blessing to be able to go home again, to ground yourself in the past by seeing the houses, schools, movie theaters and stores of your youth. But by and by, these tangible signs of personal history are swept away, along with everyday objects and ways of doing things that you have taken for granted.

The houses I grew up in are still standing but, as happened to Al Kooper, there is absolutely no vestige remaining of the Rialto, Mohawk, Regent and Tryon, the movie theaters of my youth in downtown Amsterdam.

As for common objects and practices that have been transformed, can you still buy a manual typewriter or an electric typewriter for that matter? Is there a market for adding machines that are operated by pulling a lever? Is there any company or institution with more than five employees where you speak to a human being when you first call the information number?

Why did spare tires get so small? When did they start installing locks on automobile gasoline caps? How did we know trucks were going to back up before they beeped? Do you remember before the days of personal beepers and cellular phones when you could hide from the boss, sometimes in the building but certainly when you were in the car?

Consider the folks in Brooklyn who used to be area code 212 and who now are area code 718. Long Island's long-time 516 area code now applies only to part of Long Island. Soon, our 518 area code will be split. Will we get to keep 518 or will only the people in Plattsburgh let's say, hang on to the old eastern upstate area code?

Losing the little things in life is a sure sign that, sooner or later, we are all going, going, gone.

≥≥

Bill and Dusty

Two radio entertainers who were in a league of their own

Upstate New York had two radio entertainers who, in longevity and charm, were in a league of their own. Well into their eighties, Bill Pope and Dusty Miller hosted weekly programs on WCSS, 1490 AM, in Amsterdam. Bill, who retired in 1999, did a talk show and a Big Band music program. Dusty, who died in 1998, hosted a Country and Western show. He was buried in his beautiful cowboy clothes.

A Capital District broadcasting legend, Bill Pope broke into radio at WGY in Schenectady where he did sports from 1944 to 1948. Bill's zeal for high-school sports teams added to his appeal. From 1950 to 1961, Bill was the most popular disc jockey at

Dusty Miller and his famous Colorado Wranglers

Albany's WABY. He made the transition from the pop standard music of Patti Page and Rosemary Clooney to rock-and-roll.

Bill began playing Rhythm and Blues records on Saturdays to appeal to Albany's African-American population. As other 1950s disc jockeys discovered, white teens were attracted by the music that came to be called rock-and-roll. For eleven years, Bill was the King of the Record Hops in Albany. Making a running gag out of his baldness, Bill Pope became Curly Bill. He was the disc jockey at a thousand dances. If your high school didn't book Curly Bill for the prom, you were Nowhereville.

By 1961, though, Bill thought his career as a performer had come to an end. He moved to Amsterdam to manage a radio station and sell airtime. Bill proved to be an excellent salesman but continued on the air, developing a loyal Amsterdam following. His late afternoon Rolling Home Show, which once again featured the big band sound, became a mainstay on WCSS. Later, Bill did television and radio talk in Amsterdam.

Dusty, whose real name was Elmer Rossi, always had a day job and a country band — Dusty Miller and His Famous Colorado Wranglers. The Wranglers performed on Capital District radio starting in the 1940s and had a long run at Bob's Tavern in Amsterdam in the 1960s and 1970s. Dusty usually managed to fit in a radio gig at one of Amsterdam's stations through the years and brought Amsterdam's myriad "characters" onto his WCSS program in the '90s, people ranging from bartenders to former talk hosts to country singers.

"I like country music because it shows life as it is," Dusty said, adding that a beautiful pop song like "Stardust" is a fantasy, not like the real world.

On his country show Dusty Miller sometimes played his own recordings, including his band's theme, adapted from the "Happy Roving Cowboy" — "Hear my song, as we ride along, we're the Colorado Wranglers. Herding the dark clouds out of the sky,. Keeping the heavens blue."

Bill, on his big band show, told stories about musicians and kept the show moving with his trademark self-deprecating patter: "This is Curly Bill, mikeside, starting on that second cup of coffee. Bill, no one wants to hear that, let's ask Vic Damone to step to the microphone and sing, just like this. One and two and..."

৯

Simply Fabulous
The Fab Five and the Fab Four were all celebrities

Amsterdam High's 31 consecutive basketball victories during the 1962-63 season made success appear achievable and style appear attractive.

It wasn't simply that the basketball team, coached by the energetic John Varsoke, won all those games. The players, in particular the starting team known as the Fabulous Five, were stylish. Diplomatic Gary Blongiewicz, talented Tim Kolodziej, witty Phil Schuyler, popular Dave Smith and affable Tom Urbelis were all competitive, smart, charming, graceful, funny and more than a bit irreverent as high-school students.

The fact that three of the five came from Reid Hill, where I lived until the eighth grade, made their achievements even more exciting to me.

While the Fabulous Five and their teammates were tearing up the basketball court in the early 1960s, my friends Tom Christman, Dave Dybas, Bob Lebman, Henry Madej and I sold soda at the home games. Everyone rooted for the team, including portly social studies teacher Bill Aninger, who rang a cowbell when Amsterdam scored a basket. With all the pressure and adulation, it's a wonder that the Fabulous Five kept their wits about them.

The long winning streak began during the 1961-62 season, when industrious Rick Cetnar, a senior, was captain of the team. Cetnar went on to coach basketball at Amsterdam High. He probably has felt blessed and cursed by the memory of that long-ago win-

Amsterdam High School Varsity Basketball, 1961-62; Coach John Varsoke; Rick Cetnar #20; Fabulous Five: Gary Blongiewicz #42, Tim Kolodziej #32, Phil Schuyler #34, Tom Urbelis #22, Dave Smith #40.

ning streak and the constant comparison of his old high school team to today's basketball players, at least until 1994, when the team he coached became sectional champs with his son Todd as one of the standout players.

After Cetnar graduated, Dave Smith replaced him in the starting lineup in the 1962-63 season. As part of the hoopla surrounding Amsterdam's rivalry with what was then Linton High School, sportswriter Marv Cermak in Schenectady began referring to Blongiewicz, Kolodziej, Schuyler and Urbelis as the Fearsome Foursome from Amsterdam. Smith recalls with gratitude that *Amsterdam Recorder* sportswriter Art Hoefs added Smith's name to the list when Hoefs came up with the nickname that really stuck — the Fabulous Five.

In my memory, the Fab Five of the basketball court are mixed up with the Beatles, who were known as the Fab Four in the mid-1960s. The Fab Five and the Fab Four were all celebrities.

If the British won battles because of skills learned on the playing fields of Eton, Americans who succeed in business are frequently veterans of the basketball court, football field or baseball diamond. Blongiewicz, voted best personality in high school, is in human resources and executive recruitment with an outplacement firm in the Boston area. Kolodziej lives in New Hampshire and has a key position with an insurance consulting firm. Schuyler, after a long career with the Red Cross, is now in financial services. Smith, who was president of his high school class, is an investment banker. Urbelis, voted best looking in high school, is an attorney, partner in a law firm in the Boston area.

Schuyler arranged a meeting between the Fabulous Five and Pat Riley, former Linton High basketball star and Fabulous Five opponent, then coach of the Miami Heat by way of Los Angeles and New York.

"Riley was incredibly gracious," Smith recalled. "We were reticent to infringe but he remembered everybody." Remember the Fabulous Five? How could Riley forget?

≥●

Life on Reid Hill

Growing up in Amsterdam's Polish neighborhood

I f everything important happens before puberty, then everything important in my life took place on Amsterdam's Reid Hill, the Polish neighborhood. Our family lived at 28 Pulaski Street, in Mrs. Wojcik's house, until I was in eighth grade.

Although I am not Polish, the punctuality, pride, exuberance and sadness of the Polish people became part of me. It would be be nice if Polish neatness — especially a desire for an immaculate front yard — also rubbed off, but that didn't happen.

Father Walter Czechowicz, pastor of Amsterdam's St. Stanislaus Church, said that when Poles came to Amsterdam in the late 19th and early 20th centuries, their sadness stemmed from not having a country. What is Poland today was part of three empires — Russia, Austria and Prussia.

St. Stanislaus Church was founded in 1894. Father Anton Gorski was pastor from 1895 until 1924 and again from 1931 to 1938. Local lore has it that Father Gorski, trained as a medical doctor in the old country, was smuggled out of Russian Poland in a coffin. Like many Poles, Father Gorski loved horses and organized cavalry exercises in Amsterdam. In 1897, he spearheaded efforts to build St. Stanislaus School, to this day a thriving Catholic school.

The Poles and others who lived on Reid Hill usually worked in Amsterdam's East End, at Mohawk Carpet's lower mill or other factories within walking distance. Poles who settled on Park Hill, Amsterdam's other Polish neighborhood, usually worked at the Sanford carpet mills bordering Park Hill, which was on the other side of the Chuctanunda Creek from Reid Hill.

Julia and Bob Cudmore outside their Pulaski Street home, 1952

Initially, Father Gorski was not pleased when Park Hill Poles proposed and succeeded in creating a separate Catholic parish, St. John the Baptist, founded in 1910 by pastor Peter Nowak, who served his parish family a remarkable 50 years.

One problem Park Hill Poles had in reaching St. Stanislaus was crossing the Chuctanunda Creek at the dam at Kellogg's linseed oil mill. Before the Pulaski Bridge was built over the creek in 1931, Park Hill Poles usually reached businesses, Polish clubs and salvation on Reid Hill over a rickety footbridge on the top of Kellogg's dam.

Here are some of the things I remember from Reid Hill in the 1950s:

— The newsstand at James and Hibbard Streets, where I was sent to get bread and milk, and where it was possible games of chance were occurring in the back room.

— Wytrwal's Furniture, also on Hibbard, where we looked at television in the window before we had television in our flat.

— Krupczak's Pharmacy, another Hibbard St. institution, where Lieutenant Governor Mary Ann Krupczak's career started.

— Brownie's Lunch on Reid Street, which my mother regarded as an acceptable place to get take-out food in the form of hot dogs with meat sauce.

— My parents worked and Mrs. Wojcik, our landlady, often made lunch for me: cabbage soup, golumbkis, pierogis, and the like. The substantial pierogi was the ballast that helped Poles cope with Amsterdam's harsh winters and the strenuous working conditions in the mills.

— The garden next to our house on Pulaski St., religiously tended by the elderly grandmother from the Tishko/Kawczynski house next door. "Religiously" is an appropriate word in that the garden, now a parking lot, was next door to St. Nicholas Ukrainian Catholic Church.

— DeStefano's Market, with bins of produce for sale on Jay Street. How did the DeStefanos get there? How did the Cudmores get there, for that matter, or the Ukrainians?

— The pool hall at Reid and Hibbard. I never went in. Honest.

— Listening to my friend Dave Dybas play accordion as his mother looked on with admiration at their home on Gorski street — a Reid Hill Polish kid growing up on a street named for the parish's most important pastor, taking accordion lessons and also having a bowling ball in the closet.

"That's true," Dybas said recently, after serenading a group on his accordion. "But, actually, Bob it was really no different than the Italian kids who grew up playing accordion and with a bowling ball. So we had a good time."

ﺏ

Saving Spartacus

It's hard to forget someone who has saved your life

If Wolfie Churchett hadn't acted as quickly as he did, a show business dynasty would have been stillborn. Churchett was one of my father's friends from Amsterdam's East End. His real name was Wilfred, although people called him Wolfie. Many of my father's East End friends had nicknames — Jokey, Silent Mike, Smiling Frank and Cuddy, which was what they called my father and his brothers. Like my father, Churchett's people were English immigrants.

A life-long Amsterdamian, Churchett worked as assistant engineer for the city for 25 years and was self-employed as a land surveyor until his retirement in 1976. When he died in the late 1980s, he was living with his sister Elsie at Holland Garden apartments.

In 1927, Wolfie, who was 16 at the time, saved the life of another East Ender, a younger boy who, like my father, lived on Eagle Street. Such a rescue would have been remarkable enough, but the Jewish youth that Churchett saved was unusually gifted, intellectually, artistically and physically. In a 1985 interview, the man Wolfie rescued, Issur Danielovitch Demsky, described what happened:

"I was about nine years old. The building at the end of Eagle Street near my house was undergoing construction and there was this big, five-foot deep ditch filled with water. Like a fool, I was trying to walk across on a thin board. I fell in and didn't know how to swim and was drowning when Wolfie, I can see him now, Wolfie ran up to where I was, grabbed me by the hand and pulled me out."

When Wolfie and a bedraggled Issur came to the Demsky home after the near-fatal incident, Demsky's father Harry, the local ragman, was at first distrustful of Wolfie. But Issur, whose nickname was Izzy, loudly and clearly made it known to his father that "Wolfie saved me, he saved me."

Strong like his father, young Demsky, went on to some fame as a collegiate and carnival wrestler after leaving Amsterdam. When Izzy Demsky changed his name to Kirk Douglas and embarked on a career in motion pictures, he became Amsterdam's best-known native son.

Without Wolfie's rescue of young Izzy in 1927, of course, there would have been no Kirk Douglas and, therefore, no Michael Douglas. *Lust for Life, Spartacus* and those 50 other Kirk Douglas movies, if made, would have been made by different men. There would have been no book called *The Ragman's Son* and no Lifetime Achievement Academy Award. Glenn Close would have tried to kill some actor other than Michael Douglas, Kirk Douglas's son, in *Fatal Attraction* and some actor other than Michael Douglas would have had to tell us in *Wall Street* that "Greed is good."

When Kirk Douglas visited Amsterdam through the years, he would sometimes stop to see Wolfie and they also corresponded. Douglas was generous to Wolfie in other ways as well.

In 1985, when Kirk Douglas Park was dedicated in Amsterdam, the actor made a point of telling the Wolfie Churchitt story at a press conference. Wolfie seemed surprised that Douglas did that. However, it's hard to forget someone who has saved your life.

&.

Why Amsterdam Straddles the Mighty Mohawk
How Port Jackson Became the South Side

Albanians look across the Hudson at the City of Rensselaer while Trojans view Cohoes and Watervliet on the other side of the same river. In Schenectady, if you cross the Mohawk you arrive in Scotia or Glenville. But in Amsterdam, when you drive over the Mohawk from the north side, you enter the city's South Side, that is, if you remember to leave the arterial highway before coming to the Thruway interchange. Amsterdam is the only Capital District city that straddles both sides of a major river.

In the early 1800s, what is now Amsterdam's South Side was Port Jackson, named for merchant Sam Jackson. Port Jackson was a bustling, rowdy stop on the Erie Canal, a big ditch dug from Albany to Buffalo that helped open the American West. In this part of the valley, the canal was south of the Mohawk River, bypassing Amsterdam, which was growing rapidly as a mill town north of the river.

Historian Katherine Strobeck, whose family operated a South Side lumber yard, said Port Jackson was a "wild town" boasting 14 stores and many taverns. North side Amsterdam was dry at the time. Although pictures of the Erie Canal show an idyllic form of travel, Strobeck said the canal was extremely busy — "It was just one boat after the other." There were frequent fights at the locks to see who went through first, said Strobeck, who has written the book, *Port Jackson: An Erie Canal Village.*

Port Jackson might have continued as a village in its own right but its commercial importance dwindled with the rise of the New York Central Railroad, which went through Amsterdam on the north side of the river. Most manufacturing took place north of the river, first because of the north side's powerful Chuctanunda Creek and then because of access to the railroad main line.

When Amsterdam became a city in 1885, the community had thousands of residents and was becoming a center for manufacturing carpets, brooms and other products. Amsterdam annexed Port Jackson and its 953 residents in 1888. In 1915, the Erie Canal was emptied and, in 1918, the new Barge Canal opened, using the bed of the Mohawk River.

Today, South Side access to the river — unimpeded by the railroad tracks and multi-lane highway on Amsterdam's north side — has occasioned dreams of riverfront development.

A hopeful sign says "Welcome to Port Jackson" on an access road off the South Side arterial highway.

Amsterdam's South Side has long been a stronghold for Italian-Americans, some of whom came to build stonework for the Erie Canal. With the notable exception of Chalmer's knitting mill, the

South Side has tended to be commercial and residential, kind of a suburb of the North Side.

For example, Ralph DiCaprio, an 83-year-old native South Sider, worked at four jobs in his career — a carpet mill, tire store, movie theater and card store — all north of the river. "When I was young, [the South Side] was a very vibrant community." DiCaprio said. "They had stores, they had everything. It was like a little city in itself."

Many Italian-Americans made wine, including the DiCaprio family. Neighbors entertained each other with accordions and banjos, according to DiCaprio.

"We'd just have a lot of fun," DiCaprio said. "We'd enjoy ourselves."

To this day, DiCaprio is a respected figure among bocce players who gather for regular games and regional lawn bowling tournaments at the bocce courts outside Joe Parillo's Port Jackson Deli near Bridge Street.

A World War Two veteran of Africa, Sicily and Normandy, DiCaprio has never considered leaving the South Side: "My mother and father lived here and when they passed away, I didn't want to leave. I wanted to stay with my ancestors."

ᴈ▲

What Does 50 Look Like?
Happy birthday to you

The birthdays when you turn 30, 40, 50 and 60 are often occasions for major celebrations, frequently surprise parties. When you approach those ages, remember to be on guard when your sig-

Port Jackson on the Erie Canal

nificant other disappears on a weekend night and you are sent on an important errand with a trusted friend, who suddenly finds reasons for unusual detours that usually end with the two of you walking into a crowded room.

Joe Gallagher, the impish WGY radio personality, turned 50 in 1999. After WGY colleague Don Weeks escorted Joe into the surprise party, people told Joe he doesn't look his age. Of course, many of the people telling him that are also feeling the physical effects of the passage of time: bulge around the middle, droop from the top down, difficulty hearing cocktail party conversation, the urge to sit down more often, the need to wear sensible clothes and shoes. Mentally, many of us look for signs of potential dementia in our forgetfulness, what people our age call "senior moments." Emotionally, though, we still see ourselves as young bucks and does, somehow trapped in these older bodies.

Certainly, Joe doesn't resemble the early pictures assembled by his wife, Kathy, for his surprise party. The thin-faced, longhaired guy with glasses from Joe's early days in radio has become a more square-faced and distinguished figure. However, on the radio, Joe remains a perpetual kid. I believe he always will act young on the radio, just as great painters create vigorous, exciting art works well into old age.

True, in Joe's case, his hair has turned gray. However, his hair has been gray at least since the Reagan administration. And, unlike some of us, he still has hair on his head. Also, Joe's young, active family helps keep him young. It's been a long time since my son or daughter needed to depend on dad for a ride to a sporting event, help with homework or supervision of a sleepover. The constant company of children must be stimulating, to say the least.

I passed the half-century mark some years ago. As much as it pains me to admit it, Joe Gallagher is a young-looking 50 year-old. He doesn't look a day over 49.

When the American Association of Retired Persons application came in the mail when I first turned 50, I abruptly pitched the form into the trash. However, AARP is smart enough not to give up and I keep receiving literature from them. Joining AARP increasingly seems to be a good idea, for the magazine subscription and discounts, if nothing else. That kind of thinking may be the start of the senior citizen mindset.

There are other signs of advancing age. On vacation last summer, my wife and I realized, after arriving at the restaurant, that we had gone to dinner during the early-bird special. You can't go wrong at those prices, especially if you're on a fixed income.

When young people talk with me at work or at parties, I know they are not thinking: "This man is a peer, a contemporary, a major player, a potentially significant ally, a possible threat."

At best, I'm a father figure and I am beginning to pass over into grandfather status.

There are fates worse than that.

B OB CUDMORE, author of *You Can't Go Wrong: Stories from Nero, New York and Other Tales*, is well known in Upstate New York from his work as a radio and television talk host, newspaper columnist, public relations practitioner and public speaker.

He co-produced the WMHT-TV documentary, *Amsterdam: Historic Views of the Carpet City*.

A native of Amsterdam, Cudmore hosted WGY radio's popular night-time talk show Contact from 1980 to 1993. Since 1993, he has worked in public relations at the State University of New York System Administration in Albany. He is an adjunct professor in the Department of Public Communications at the College of St. Rose.

He has written a regular column for *The Record* newspaper and contributed articles to the *Daily Gazette, Times-Union* and *The Recorder;* hosted call-in segments on WTEN-TV; anchored newscasts at several radio stations; done dramatic readings with the Schenectady Symphony Orchestra; and contributed articles to *Talkers,* the radio talk show trade magazine.

He earned an M.A. and B.A. in English from Boston University.

A resident of Glenville, New York, Cudmore's family includes his wife, Mary, a trainer for Weight Watchers International, and two grown children: Bob Cudmore, Jr., of Somerville, Massachusetts, and Kathleen R. Cudmore of Schenectady, New York.

Jeanne A. Benas, cartoonist and illustrator, is a graduate of Syracuse University, where she earned a BFA degree. She began her own business after working in a variety of commercial art capacities. Benas Art Studio creates humorous and realistic illustrations for books, magazines and political/editorial articles, with clients throughout the country. She was recently named one of the "Prominent Women of the Capital District." She lives in Latham, New York, with her husband, Richard, and son, Adam, and Dachshund, Sneakers.

ORDER FORM

You Can't Go Wrong: Stories from Nero, New York and Other Tales

SOFTCOVER   Quantity _____ @ $11.95 each = _____

HARDCOVER   Quantity _____ @ $16.95 each = _____
— *WITH AUTHOR'S SIGNATURE*

AUDIOBOOK   Quantity _____ @ $16.95 each = _____
— *STORIES READ BY THE AUTHOR AND FEATURING*
THE SONG MY OLD TOWN *AND MUSICAL*
INTERLUDES BY JOHN SCIOLINO
AND NOR'EASTER

Subtotal   _____

Shipping   _____
$3 (US) for the first
book or audio book
and $1.50 for each
additional product.

Visit the Nero
web site at
bobcudmore.com

Sales Tax   _____
Add 7.75% for
products shipped to
New York State.

Total   _____

Make checks payable to **Nero Publishing Company,** *and send to Nero Publishing Company, PMB 107, 123 Saratoga Road, Glenville, New York 12302*

Name: _____

Address: _____

City:_____

State: _____ Zip Code: _____

Telephone:_____

E-mail address: _____